McMillan - Mary-Anne thi

Christy

Christy

BY CAROLE BOLTON

WILLIAM MORROW AND COMPANY
NEW YORK

Grateful acknowledgment is made for permission to quote from *September Song:* Copyright © 1938 by DeSylva, Brown and Henderson, Inc.

To Grace Darling

Christy

Chapter 1

I have decided to write the story of my life. Whatever I turn out to be in my later years, I do have a very strong feeling that I am going to be something interesting, and it is never too early to write an autobiography for the sake of posterity.

I was born sixteen years ago, right here in Peabody. It's just a little college town of no particular importance, although I suppose a lot of people would say it was picturesque because of the lake and the mountains in the distance and all, but it's really very dull—or was until recently.

Ralph and Edna Collier, my parents, have only one child—me. Daddy is in the real-estate business. He has a little pot belly, and his hair is getting thin on top. Mother looks quite young to have a daughter my age, and there is no gray in her dark hair. They are pretty nice, as parents go. They are very modern and have a good sense of humor, although they don't always understand me.

My name is Christine, but everyone calls me Christy. It's hard to describe what I look like without sounding conceited, but I have been told that I'm pretty when I'm dressed up—or I would be pretty if I didn't have Problem Hair. It's fair like my father's, and early last summer I still wore it long, in a pony tail most of the time. When I try to curl my hair, it just sticks out in all directions like a half-plucked chicken.

I might as well skip the first part of my life, because nothing happened then, aside from the usual childhood diseases and an infantile crush on a boy in the eighth grade. I really feel that my life never even began until Gideon Myles came into it—last June. It was a Saturday afternoon, and I had just been cleaning my room. Mother made me do it; she said that every time she went into it she got a terrible shock.

Once I get started on it, I really enjoy cleaning my room. I like taking out the books and dusting each one, and sometimes I find that I've been sitting on the floor for hours looking over old books that I haven't glanced at for years. On this particular Saturday I had gotten well into *The Little Minister* when Mother came in and raised Cain. So I reluctantly put the book away, finished the dusting, and started on the drawers. They were very discouraging. Old school notebooks, pencils, souvenirs, and snapshots were all mixed up with slips, panties, socks, and nylons. Photography was my hobby a long time ago, and it was fun to linger over the old pictures. There was one of a blue jay sitting on a tree limb that I really began to wish I had sent off to a contest, because it was quite good. I had managed to get very close to him, and he had his beak open in a ludicrous way. The only thing I ever had to take pictures with was an old box camera that went on Mother and Daddy's honeymoon with them. Unfortunately, however, I dropped it down a quarry when I was on a hike one day, and it never was any good after that, and they wouldn't buy me another one, because they said I was too careless. That ended my career in photography.

I was lovingly piling the snapshots in a little stack when Mother came in again, this time with the vacuum cleaner.

"Christy, what in the world are you doing?"

"Cleaning out my drawers. I'm finished now."

"I could clean the whole house in the time it takes you to do this one room," she said.

After I had vacuumed the room and put the cleaner away I got out some curlers and put up my hair and hoped it would look better than it usually did, because I had a date with Barry Preston that night. Anyway, I knew Mother would have a fit if I went anywhere with the pony tail. She was always after me to have it cut and get a permanent, but I always preferred to look casual. I felt more comfortable that way.

When my hair was up in curlers I went downstairs to get something to eat. Nora had just cleaned the kitchen, and the floor was sparkling with wax. I opened the refrigerator door.

"Oh no, Christy," said Nora. "Your mother says you're not to get a lot of food out and mess up the kitchen. Anyway, it isn't too long since you had lunch."

"Well, I can have an orange, for goodness' sake," I said.

I sliced the orange in half on the sink and made a big fuss over wiping off the drainboard afterward, but Nora just smiled at me as I walked toward the living room sucking on half of the orange. Fate was coming into my life then, but I didn't know it. As I went out into the hall I could see the front walk through the screen door. A man had stopped there and was looking at the sign, which says *Ralph Collier, Real Estate and Insurance*. Then he turned up the walk. Since the hall was dim he couldn't see me, so he rang the bell. Not suspecting what was ahead of me, I answered the door—and just

thinking about it, I could *die!* There I was in my old
faded and frayed jeans, and the old shirt of Daddy's that
I was wearing was dusty from my books. I had my hair
up in those awful fat curlers, and to top it all I was sucking on that orange half and squeezing juice into my
mouth, just like an *infant*.

The disgusting part of it was that I hardly cared at
all that a stranger should see me like this.

"Yes?" I said, through the screen.

"Could I see Mr. Collier? I'd like to talk to him about
this ad in the paper." He held it up and pointed to a
classified ad that had been circled in ink.

"Daddy!" I yelled. "It's for you."

And then I stood there and stared at him with the
worst possible manners. I didn't know at that time what
he was going to mean to me.

Since he had the light in back of him I couldn't see
him very well—he probably had a better look at me, I'm
afraid—but I got a general impression of tallness and
healthy bronzed blondness.

Daddy came out of his office at the right of the hall
as you face the porch. "Yes?" he said. "Come in,
please."

The stranger entered and I stood aside to let him
pass. In the office doorway Daddy got a good look at
him, and I heard him say, "Well, I'll be—! It isn't possible. Gideon Myles!"

Gideon Myles stopped and stared back at him. "Why, you really are Ralph Collier. You know, when I was looking at that sign outside I wondered if it could be the same person."

"It is! It is!" Daddy said jovially. "Well, if this doesn't beat everything. You old son of a gun, you."

The next thing they were shaking hands and thumping each other on the back as if they were crazy. Through all their excited talk and laughter, I remembered that they had gone to Peabody College at the same time. I had heard Daddy brag a lot of times about Gideon Myles, the local boy who had made good. His mother had died right after he graduated, and he had left town never to come back. No one would have remembered him at all if he hadn't become a writer, quite a successful one, in fact. I had never bothered to read any of his books myself, but Daddy had read them all, because he had known the author. And now I could see that he was tickled pink to have Gideon here in the flesh to show off in front of me.

"What are you doing back in the old burg?" he said.

Gideon flourished the newspaper again. "I want to buy a place up by the lake. The last few years I've been getting sort of homesick for the old scenes and I thought it might be nice to have a little place up there I could come back to from time to time."

"Well, boy, I think that's wonderful," said Daddy,

in his best Chamber of Commerce style. "You've been all over the world, but when you come right down to it, there's no place like home."

"I have a nice little apartment in New York," Gideon said. "I just thought that maybe a few months out of the year. . . ." Again he pointed to the newspaper. "How about this ad you have in the paper? 'Three-room lake cottage, five isolated acres, six thousand dollars.'"

Daddy glanced at the paper contemptuously. "Oh, you wouldn't want that," he said. "It's awfully run down. Don't worry. We'll find you something. First, though, I want you to meet my family. This is my daughter, Christy. She isn't looking her best right now, but when her face is washed, she can be quite the young lady."

I felt like hiding under something at that remark, but I just smiled weakly and hid the orange behind my back.

Gideon grinned, his teeth gleaming in his sunburned face. He held out his hand, but I backed away hurriedly. There was half an orange in each of my hands and both of them were sticky, too. I would have died rather than touch him with such paws, and I began to sidle toward the stairway.

"Christy," Daddy said, not noticing my discomfort at all, "go get your mother. She'll want to meet Gideon."

I was glad to get away, and as soon as Mother went downstairs, I rushed into the bathroom and washed my face and hands and took the curlers out of my hair. Although I toyed with the idea of changing into a dress, I decided it would look too obvious if I suddenly appeared downstairs in a different outfit. I didn't stop then to wonder why I cared how I looked to Gideon, but now I realize that that grin of his had been my undoing—the grin and the broad shoulders and the crisp stubby hair bleached by the sun. He was not exactly handsome, but there was something dashing about him. His blue eyes had sparkled at me like no blue eyes I had ever seen before, and there was a youthfulness in them, perhaps because, not being held down to a job like most men, he looked at the world all the time as though it were always something new and exciting. And he had glamour, because he was famous—at least, a little bit famous—and I knew he had traveled. I had never met anyone glamorous before.

It was hard to believe he was in the same generation as Daddy, although, to be accurate, he had been a freshman at college when Daddy was a senior.

I tiptoed down the stairs. They were all in the office, so I stood at the door. They were so busy talking that they didn't notice me at all. I heard Daddy say, "Where are you staying, Gideon?"

"At the hotel."

"That's right, you lost your mother, didn't you? But haven't you any friends or relatives in town?"

"Not any more. The relatives moved away to more industrial areas, and I'm afraid I've been too busy traveling to keep up with my friends after all these years."

"Well, we can't have you staying at the hotel."

"It's very comfortable, really," Gideon said. He was sitting on the desk with his arms folded. "You should see some of the places where I've had to stay in different parts of the world."

"I can imagine. But just the same, we can't have you staying at a hotel in the town where you were born and grew up. I have it! You stay with us until you find your cottage. We have a nice guest room. Don't you think that would be best, Edna?"

Mother agreed, but I thought Gideon looked uncomfortable. "That's very nice of you, Ralph, but I prefer the hotel. Besides, I don't want to put you out."

That was the wrong way to put it. He should have said he preferred the hotel and let it go at that, for Daddy insisted. "Nonsense. It's no trouble. We'd consider it an honor. As soon as we see the house I want to show you this afternoon, we'll go over to the hotel and get your bags and check you out."

"No, really—" Gideon looked definitely unhappy by this time, but Daddy considered the matter settled and obviously thought Gideon was only making polite sounds. He had gotten out some lists from his files and was looking them over. Mother said nothing, but I could see she knew how Gideon felt. I saw her meet his eyes behind Daddy's back, and then shrug and raise her eyebrows to the ceiling in a helpless way. Gideon grinned at her, and this time my heart did turn over. I was sorry he didn't want to stay with us, but I was very glad he was going to. I could have hugged Daddy for being so blindly and insistently hospitable.

After Daddy and Gideon left to look at the house, I got into a dress and dashed over to the library. There were quite a few books by Gideon Myles on the shelves, and I picked out the one with the most recent copyright. Julie Fanelle and Emma Morrison, the librarians, were both at the loan desk, and as I knew Julie might make comments about my choice, I shoved the book toward Emma. It did no good, though. Emma was often bitten by the same inquisitive bug.

Idly she glanced at the card as she removed it from the pocket. "My goodness, Christy," she said, "why do you want to read this?"

Craning her neck, Julie looked over her shoulder. "Gideon Myles? I should hope not," she said.

"What's wrong with his books?" I asked.

"Trash," Emma said, with a look of distaste. "Sheer trash."

"His books are in the library," I observed innocently. "Someone must have bought them."

Julie gave Emma a grin, but the veteran librarian was unmoved by it. "We have to appeal to all sorts of tastes," she said. "Anyway, he's harmless enough—for adult readers."

She fixed me with a stern stare, and I looked down at the book and waited stubbornly.

"What brought this on anyhow?" Julie asked, taking the book from Emma and stamping it for me.

I figured I might as well tell her; she would find out soon enough. "Because," I said, "he's in town looking for a lake cottage to buy. Daddy latched on to him this afternoon and talked him into staying with us."

"Why, Christy! How exciting!"

"Um," said Emma. "Is that so? Well, I remember him when he used to come in here. A brash, overconfident boy, if I ever saw one."

"He's very nice," I said indignantly.

"I'm sure he is, darling." Julie handed me the book, smiling broadly. "And don't worry about Miss Morrison. If I know her, she's probably wondering right now how she can persuade him to come in here to visit for old time's sake."

"Indeed!" the older woman exclaimed, but she looked a little less severe as she exchanged an amused glance with Julie.

And this seems like a good place to explain about Julie. She is my mother's best friend—and also one of mine. It isn't strange that she is, because she comes sort of between us in age. As long as I can remember, Julie has always been around, guiding my reading, taking me to the movies when I was broke, lending me money, and listening to my secrets. Sometimes she's acted as a kind of mediator between me and Mother. Because of her combination of youth and maturity, she has often been able to explain us to each other.

Julie isn't married, and it's a mystery to me that no man has grabbed her up. She keeps house beautifully for her father, and she is warm and lovable. Daddy says she is too smart for the men in Peabody. Men, he says, don't like a woman who seems to know more than they do. But I notice that he's very glad when she occasionally comes over in the evening to type for him and that the work often ends with him sitting on her desk laughing with her. Daddy isn't scared of Julie.

I once had quite a crush on Julie, the kind of crush a younger girl gets on an older girl she admires, and a flash of it came back as she leaned over the desk with her good-natured smile.

"Incidentally, Christy," she said, "there's someone I want you to meet. My cousin Frank just arrived in town this morning. He's going to be staying with us."

I must have looked blank, for she said, "Don't you

remember? I told you about him. Starting Monday, he's going to work here in the library for the summer, and next fall he'll go to Peabody College. I know he isn't as thrilling as your house guest," she added wickedly, "but I'm sure you're going to like him."

Frank Fanelle had absolutely no interest for me at that moment, but I promised Julie I'd come in Monday and see what he looked like. Then, taking my book, I went back home, wound my hair up in the curlers again, and spent the rest of the afternoon reading Gideon's book, which was called *Flight from Danger*. It was about this newspaper correspondent in Hong Kong at the time the Communists took over China. He's sort of worthless and spends all his time drinking in quaint little bars until he learns that a girl he has once loved is stranded way up in Red territory, and goes to rescue her. It's very exciting and has a lot of good description in it and one terrific love scene where they are hiding in a clump of bushes while these soldiers march by. I didn't have time to read all of it then, but later that night I stayed up after the movies to finish it in bed.

Chapter 2

It was easy to tell when Daddy came back with Gideon, because I heard them bringing his luggage upstairs to the guest room. I streaked into the bathroom before he could see me, and took a shower and then put on another dress and brushed my hair. The haphazard curling hadn't done much good, but it did at least leave it sort of wavy-looking.

Then I went down to help Mother get dinner, as Nora had gone for the day.

"What are you doing in those clothes?" she asked, and I wished she wouldn't talk so loud.

"Margo and I have a double date tonight with Barry and Steve."

"It's for after dinner, isn't it? You could have waited until then to put on your best dress."

"I want to look nice, since we have company," I said, putting on an apron. "It's exciting to have a famous author in the house."

"I don't know how famous he is," said Mother.

"Don't you like him, for goodness' sake?"

"How could I help it? He's quite captivating." Mother smiled, and the smile made her look very young. "Even so," she added quickly, "I don't think your father should have pressed him so hard to stay. He was probably much happier at the hotel, where he could come and go as he liked. We must try to make him feel at home. It might be a good idea to invite Julie Fanelle over while he's here."

"Why?" I asked, getting suspicious.

Mother had a bad habit of always inviting eligible bachelors to the house to meet Julie, but much as I loved her, it seemed unwise to me to push her on a man like Gideon Myles. However, Mother just looked smug. "I think Julie would enjoy meeting him. After all, she does work with books," she said.

"Is Mr. Myles married?" I asked carefully.

"No, he isn't," said Mother.

I tried to keep my eyes off Gideon during dinner, but it was hard to do, especially as he was telling us about one of his adventures in that slow sophisticated drawl of his.

"Well, there I was," he said, "stranded in Rio without any money. I had to do something, so I joined an expedition going into the interior. The photographer had gotten sick, so I took over his job, although I didn't know much about photography at the time."

"Oh," I said excitedly, "are you interested in photography?"

"Interested or not, I certainly knew a lot about it when that trip was over."

"Say," put in Daddy, "isn't it in Brazil that they have those *piranha* fish that eat men and animals alive?"

"Ralph," said Mother, making a face, "do we have to discuss things like that at the table?"

"Well, it isn't a very pretty story," said Gideon, "but as a matter of fact, one of our Indians fell into a stream full of those devils. He was crossing over on a log and slipped—cut his foot on a jagged twig, and the surprise made him lose his balance. The poor beggar didn't last long. To my dying day I'll never forget it." Then Gideon glanced over at Mother, who was looking slightly green. "I think Edna's right. This isn't a very appetizing subject for dinner."

"They have army ants down there too, don't they?" Daddy persisted.

"Yes," said Gideon. "All kinds of ants, as well as

mosquitoes and heat. It can be pretty itchy," he added dryly. "The first thing I did when I got back to Rio was to soak in a bathtub for half a day."

He was leaning back in his chair with his hand curled around his coffee cup; and sitting there with the smoke from his cigarette rising in a straight line from his other hand, he looked the very picture of urbanity. Yet I could imagine him in the jungle, too, with his shirt open at the neck, and perspiration beading his sunburned forehead, and the muscles in his arms bulging as he hacked his way through the thick green growth with his machete. Then I noticed that Mother was watching me with a sort of rueful little smile on her face, and I got up quickly and started clearing my place at the table.

"I guess I'll go and start the dishes," I said.

"Oh, I'm sorry," said Gideon. "Am I holding you up?"

"No, no! Take your time. The ones in the kitchen will keep me busy for a while."

As I left the room I heard Daddy saying fondly, "Christy has a date tonight with a nice young boy in her class. I guess she wants to get through her chores." His tone was just plain patronizing; it made me cringe. Suddenly Barry seemed awfully juvenile to me.

This feeling became even more acute when Barry himself—freshly crew-cut and with a clean, shiny face—arrived promptly at eight. Usually when I have a date

I make the boy wait for me awhile so he won't think I'm anxious. Although I'm always dressed and ready, I sit on my bed for five minutes and then go down to him, but tonight I was waiting at the door.

"Come on," I said. "Let's go, or we'll never make the next show."

Barry seemed surprised that I was ready and, I think, a little flattered. He's really a very nice boy, and until that night, the greatest thing that could happen to me was a date with him. He is tall and clean-cut and makes good marks in school, not to mention being on the football team. His family is one of the best in Peabody, and any girl who has a date with him can really feel that she has arrived, as far as school is concerned.

But just the same, when I saw him standing there on the porch that night I wanted more than anything else to turn right around and go up to my room and pretend I had never met him.

Mother came out into the hall. "Why, hello, Barry," she said, and looked at me. "Aren't you going to ask Barry in for a minute?" she asked me.

"We'll be late," I said. "Margo and Steve are waiting for us down at her house."

"Oh," said Mother. "Well, good night then, Barry. Have a good time, children, and don't stay out too late."

I was glad to get out of that, for I felt I would die if Gideon met him and saw how young he was. Relieved, I opened the screen door and went out, and as I went I heard Mother dialing the phone in the office.

"Hello," she said softly. "Julie?"

My relief changed to a feeling of annoyance that she should waste so little time in calling up Julie. Why did married women get such a compulsion to marry off all their friends? I vowed I would never be so presumptuous when I was married. No one wanted to see Julie married more than I did, but she was not Gideon's type at all.

What was Gideon's type? That was an interesting speculation. Someday I was sure I would be, but not quite yet. . . . I was too young. How horrible it was to be young! At least Julie had maturity in her favor. And in that moment, Julie, whom I had always adored, became a rival, simply because she was almost twice my age.

I'm afraid I wasn't very talkative on the way to Margo's house. And when we reached there I caught an unexpected glimpse of myself in the hall mirror. The way you probe a sore spot in your mouth with your tongue, I wanted to probe my face, torturing myself with its lack of distinction. I hadn't even lived yet, and it showed in my face. It showed in all our faces.

Margo came out of the living room holding hands with Steve. Her short hair, like a black cap, followed the contours of her head in a way that looked French and cute, and she had on her navy-blue dress with the Chinese collar, which she thinks is so sophisticated. And she did look sophisticated in a way, but it was only superficial. She really looked very young, with her dancing eyes and her giggle. All of us looked young, and the only one who minded it was me.

"Hi, Christy," she said, and her eyes telegraphed to me her joy that she had a date with Steve and I had one with Barry, for this was the thing we had finally managed with a great deal of intrigue and planning. "What's the matter?" she whispered when she had a chance.

"Nothing," I said. "I'll tell you later—tomorrow."

Fortunately she didn't press the matter. Instead, she took Steve's arm, and the four of us went on to the movies.

Chapter 3

On Sunday morning I overslept and wasn't able to go
to Sunday school, but I did go to church with Mother
and Daddy, and Gideon went with us. I would have
been embarrassed to have people stare at me the way
they did at him, but he just smiled at them in an easy
natural way and nodded his head in a sort of little bow.
He sat next to me in the pew, and we shared a hymnbook. I was so nervous at having him beside me that I
could hardly sing, although he sang well in a steady,
confident baritone. When Margo came down the aisle
with the choir I saw her glance at me and then she did
a double-take and twisted her head around to stare back,
all bug-eyed, forgetting to sing. I smiled demurely, and

after that I was able to sing a little louder. But all through the service I was conscious of Gideon there on my right, with the smell of his shaving lotion in my nostrils—a sort of spicy outdoorsy scent.

Later, after church, I went out on the porch to read the Sunday papers, and found Gideon already there, sitting on the swing with his hands behind his head in a musing attitude. I had been wanting to talk to him without anyone else around and here was my chance, only I couldn't think of anything to say. My hands were perspiring as I picked up the paper and sat down on the steps with it and acted as though I were interested in the magazine section.

Gideon came over and sat down beside me, glancing at the paper.

"*Genes and Radioactivity*," he read aloud. "Are you interested in science, Christy?"

"Oh, I like to keep well informed. This is something that should interest everybody, I think."

"You're right there."

He looked across the street, where old Mr. Middleton was asleep in his rocking chair under an oak tree. "I'd forgotten," he said, "how sleepy a small American town can be on Sunday."

"It can be a living death," I said fervently.

"What do you do for fun?"

"Oh, I read a lot," I replied, "and sometimes we ride

our bikes or go skating. It's sort of childish, but there really isn't much else to do. Of course we go swimming in the lake, although it's still pretty cold right now."

"Yes, the lake. As a matter of fact, that's what drew me here. I've seen a lot of places in my travels, but there's something about the scenes where you grew up. . . ." He broke off and lit a cigarette. "It's always seemed to me," he said, "that no lake was ever as cold or as clear as that one. Once, during the war in the Sahara, my buddies and I ran out of water when we got separated from our platoon. I thought of the lake then and vowed I'd come back one day if I could."

"And now you're here," I said softly.

"Yes. I can hardly believe it. There's something rather unreal about the town, though, you know."

"In what way?"

"Everything seems brighter and more lucid than I remember it. Smaller, too."

"I guess it would seem smaller," I said, and I felt a sudden thrill, for I realized that we were holding a conversation and that it wasn't difficult at all. "It must seem terribly dull after all those places you've been to and the things you've done. Weren't you bored last night?"

"Last night?"

"Yes," I said carefully. "Didn't Mother have . . . some people in?"

Gideon laughed out loud. "No, that's scheduled for tonight," he said.

"I'm so sorry for you."

"Well, don't be. I really do enjoy it. I like people, you know."

And I saw that what he said was true. He did like people. His pleasantness at church had not been put on; it was genuine. Now he was even being pleasant to me, who must seem just a little girl to him.

"Is that what makes you a writer? Liking people, I mean?"

"It could be," he said, "although I must admit that I'm not really a very good writer."

"Oh, that isn't true! I read one of your books last night, and I couldn't sleep until I finished it. I never read anything so real."

"Which one was it?"

"Flight from Danger."

He grinned to himself. "That one paid for a very lovely vacation in Jamaica." But then he frowned. "Young girls like you shouldn't be reading trash like that."

"You shouldn't write trash then," I retorted, "if that's what you think it is. Besides, I've read a lot worse books than that."

"I'll bet your father didn't know."

"They were his books," I said, and laughed. "But no, he didn't know."

Daddy chose just that moment to come out on the porch. "Who didn't know what?" he asked.

Gideon winked at me. "We were just talking about books," he said.

"Oh," said Daddy. He picked the papers up off the step, sat down with a grunt, and leafed through them.

"Here are the funnies, Christy. Do you want them?"

"No! I hate funnies."

Daddy gave a laugh that was more like a snort, and I turned around and glared at him. However, he was already absorbed in the sports section, with his glasses on his nose and looking just too middle-class for words. I couldn't hold back a sigh, and Daddy looked at me over his glasses. "What's the matter with you?"

"Nothing," I said with dignity.

Daddy looked at Gideon. "Edna is fixing a lunch," he said. "After that we'll go look at a couple of houses, Gideon."

"Can I go, Daddy?" I asked.

"No, honey. You'd just get in the way. This is business."

"It's all right with me if she goes," said Gideon, and I gave him a grateful look.

"She'll have forgotten all about it by then," Daddy said, crackling the paper.

"I won't either," I persisted.

"Christy!" said Daddy with a warning note in his voice.

"Oh, all right!" I got up and went into the house. It was a temptation to slam the screen, although of course I didn't, but I just couldn't sit there any longer and be treated like a child in front of Gideon.

In the darkness of the hall, though, I turned around and looked outside. Daddy had gone back to his paper, and Gideon was just sitting there where I had left him, leaning back against the porch pillar. He looked, I thought, just like an ad in *The New Yorker*. The sun was shining on his hair as he stared pensively out into the street, but for all the stillness of his posture, there was a sense of life and energy about him waiting to be unleashed.

Swiftly I whirled and ran up the steps to my room, where I threw myself on the bed, overwhelmed by the thoughts and emotions that were suddenly crowding over me. Something had happened to me almost from the first moment Gideon had come into the house yesterday, and now I was beginning to have a word for it. The word was *love*. All at once it had a new meaning for me, and I could see what they are trying to say in books when they talk about it. It can't be described really. It is something that comes all over you and colors everything you see or do or think or feel. I was in love with Gideon, and it was as if I had never been alive before.

I had had crushes on boys in my life. Why, just last week Margo and I had been overcome by emotion at the thought of finally going out with Barry and Steve. But that was just kid stuff. This feeling I suddenly had for Gideon was something new in my experience. It was as though I had passed from one room into another, where a blue light was burning instead of the pink one I had left behind.

After lunch Gideon and Daddy left for the rest of the day, and I found myself with an afternoon on my hands. Usually Margo and I have something planned for Sunday, but we hadn't had a chance to talk about it the night before. I guess that we had previously hoped the boys would suggest something for the day, but they didn't. However, I knew she'd probably drop in after a while. Meanwhile, I read the papers, concentrating on the front pages and the article Gideon had admired me for reading, and then I figured I might just as well read the funnies, too.

When the phone rang, Mother called down for me to answer it, so I did, and a coy female voice on the other end informed me that she was Hettie Bliss of the society page of the *Peabody Times*.

"A little bird told me you had Mr. Gideon Myles, the author, staying at your house," she chirped.

"Yes," I said noncommittally, wondering just how much I should tell her.

She wanted to know if he was the same Gideon Myles who had lived in Peabody as a boy, and I said he was, and then she asked how long he would be here, and I said I didn't know.

"Well, surely there will be some doings at your house while you have such a well-known visitor. I know my readers would love to know about them and who's going to be invited."

I gave up at that and called Mother, and, with my hand over the receiver, told her it was a reporter. Mother looked flustered, for we Colliers are not frequent items on the society page, but she rose to the bait well. I could see she was enjoying herself as she talked to Hettie.

"Just a few people tonight," I heard her say, as I returned to my funny papers, and then she mentioned the names of a couple who were family friends, as well as Julie and Frank Fanelle.

"Frank Fanelle's that cousin of Julie's, isn't he?" I asked when she hung up.

"Yes," Mother said. "He just came to town yesterday. He'll be staying with the Fanelles for a while. In the fall he's supposed to start his first year at Peabody

College, but meanwhile, Julie says, he's going to spend the summer helping out in the library to make some money toward his expenses."

"That's nice," I said, but I already knew that, and I wasn't very much interested in Julie's cousin.

"Julie wanted to bring him over tonight so he could meet you," Mother said, trying a little too hard to be casual about it.

"Why me, for heaven's sake? Has every female over six been bitten by the matchmaking bug?"

"No one's trying to matchmake you, darling," Mother said, pulling my pony tail. "You're much too young. Now go upstairs and put some curlers in your hair so you'll look nice tonight."

"I can't. Margo's coming over."

"Margo won't mind."

"We might want to go somewhere."

Just then Margo suddenly rode up to the curb in front of the house on her bike.

"Hi!" she yelled.

"See?" I said to Mother, and ran down to meet her.

Margo didn't get off the bike, but just braced herself with one foot on the curb. She folded her arms and looked at me reproachfully. "And you didn't say one thing last night," she accused me.

"About what?"

"You know very well what. Gideon Myles. That was him in church with you, wasn't it?"

I nodded.

"I nearly flipped when I saw that gorgeous creature holding on to your hymnbook. All through church I nearly died of curiosity, but by the time I got my robe off, you were gone. My best friend! And I had to ask somebody else who he was."

"I couldn't talk about it last night."

"Why not? The boys would have been awfully impressed."

"Would they?" I asked doubtfully.

"Well, it certainly would have been better to talk about him than the way you did act. You were a perfect stick last night, Chris."

"I didn't think I was."

"Something was the matter with you," she said. "You certainly weren't your usual self."

"I thought I was all right. . . . I tried to be."

I stood pondering beside her bike. I was filled with two conflicting emotions. Part of me wanted to bare my soul to Margo, to tell her what had happened to me and describe this thunderbolt. I wanted to hear my voice speaking his name. Another part of me backed away from such revelations. Gideon was too wonderful, too perfect to be the topic of conversation between two schoolgirls. That part of me wanted to keep him all to myself as something too holy to be spoken of, even to Margo.

She rattled the handle bars of the bike impatiently. "Well, anyway," she said, "tell me about Gideon Myles. Is he as fascinating as he looks?"

"Oh, yes," I said in a cautious voice. "He's very interesting."

"Interesting! I thought you'd be raving about him. I even came up here today to give you a chance to gloat over him, and all you can say is that he's interesting."

"Well, he is," I defended myself. "He tells marvelous stories about jungles and deserts. I guess he must have been all over the world. Well, anyhow, you'll probably get a chance to meet him, and you can decide for yourself."

"When can I meet him?"

"I don't know. I'll tell you when. Tonight wouldn't do. Mother's invited some people over."

Margo got back on the seat of the bike. "Well, don't you forget."

"You're not going home already, are you?"

"I've got to. We've got company—some little kids are there, and Mother says I have to entertain them. I wouldn't inflict them on you—unless you'd like it," she added hopefully.

"No. I'm not in the mood for kids."

"Neither am I," said Margo sourly, "but I'd better go.

Mother said I could only stay five minutes. Want to ride up to the lake tomorrow?"

"Maybe. I'll see," I said, not wanting to commit myself to anything while Gideon was in the house. "Call me in the morning and I'll tell you then."

"Sure," she said and then added, with a gleam in her eye, "Maybe *he'll* answer the phone."

"Well, if he does, don't *gush* over him, or he'll think *we're* little kids," I told her firmly.

"You should know me better than that," she said and, imitating the voice of Marlene Dietrich, whose records we had often listened to, she said, "I'm a woman of the world. I can't halp it." She giggled then like a child of ten and peddled off after making a U turn in the street. I watched her fondly. Margo can be very silly, but I love her dearly.

I watched until she turned up the drive at her house a few doors down the street, and then I went back to the porch, feeling satisfied. I hadn't told her, and she hadn't guessed. I hoped I could keep it that way. If I could fool Margo I could fool anybody, and no one would know how much in love I was with Gideon.

Mother told me I *had* to put up my hair, and I was too engrossed in daydreams of Gideon to make a fuss about it. As I stared absently at myself in the bathroom mirror, I imagined myself about four years older and just married to Gideon. I saw us on the train to New York and then getting on one of those big ships with swimming pools and stores and movie theaters on them. We would go to Europe—Paris with Gideon! How wonderful that would be! Perhaps we would ride on the Orient Express. I imagined a mysterious man in the compartment with us. He would have a small package which he guarded carefully, and then, just before he died (he was murdered), he would ask us to deliver the package for him in Istanbul. The Orient Express did start in Paris and go to Istanbul, didn't it? I would have to look that up.

And then the most wonderful idea hit me! I knew how I could make myself interesting to Gideon. It wasn't enough just to love and admire him. I had to have something in common with him, and what could be more logical than to become a writer? I could picture us after our marriage traveling all over the world, writing together and criticizing each other's work.

I went to my room and got one of my old school notebooks and started a story that very afternoon, sitting at Mother's secretary in the living room. It was very hard to think of an opening sentence, especially as I wasn't sure of what I was going to write about or how I would end it, but I felt sure I could think it up as I went along.

Finally I got a picture in my mind and put down the

opening words. "It was raining when Peter and Penny Miller left Paris on the Orient Express for the second lap of their honeymoon. When they reached the train, steam was already rising warningly from the impatient engine. A little conductor with a mustache shouted—"

"What are you doing?" Mother inquired, as she came into the living room.

"Nothing," I said, covering the page.

"Surely you don't have homework over the summer vacation."

"Of course not," I said. "If you must know, I'm writing a story."

"Really? Why, I think that's wonderful. What's it about?"

"Well, I'm not sure, except that it's a spy story that takes place on the Orient Express."

"Where did you get an idea like that? I should think you'd want to write about something you're more familiar with."

"I'm not familiar with anything, that's the trouble," I said. "And nothing ever happens around here."

"It did yesterday. Gideon came."

I looked at her sharply, but her face was bland. Did she suspect anything? No, that was impossible. Even Margo hadn't.

"How do you say, 'All aboard,' in French?" I asked.

"I don't know," she said. "You're the one who's taking high-school French."

There was a pause. I wished she would leave me alone, but she hovered around. "What made you suddenly get it into your head to write stories?" she asked.

"I think I may have a talent for it."

"It's possible," she said, but I could see she really didn't think so. Parents never think their children can do anything, it seemed to me. My parents never encouraged me in anything, and I thought of the camera.

"Mother," I said suddenly, "could you advance me some allowance?"

Mother pursed her lips. "What for?"

"I want to buy a camera. I already have five dollars of my own to put toward one, and I want to get a fairly good one."

"I thought you were saving for a new bathing suit."

A struggle went on inside me. A bathing suit to make me look attractive to Gideon, or a camera, which I had really wanted for ages and which would give us something more in common? Which would it be?

"My old bathing suit is still pretty good. I don't actually need one this year."

Mother smiled approvingly. "Now you're showing the proper attitude, Christy. As a matter of fact, I've felt rather guilty about the camera."

"What do you mean?"

"Well, you did seem interested in photography once, and I've felt that we weren't encouraging you enough, because we didn't buy you a new one. But you never mentioned it again after that one Christmas, and you never made the slightest effort to save for one yourself. I thought you'd lost interest, since you weren't willing to make a sacrifice."

"But I didn't. I just sort of forgot about it," I said. "Yesterday, looking over those old pictures in my drawer, I remembered again."

"Good. I like to see you interested in something like photography, and it seems to me you're old enough to take better care of a camera now. If you're willing to use your own money for part of the cost, your father and I will be glad to pay the rest."

"Oh, Mother, thanks! Can I get it tomorrow?"

"I suppose so," she said, smiling.

Satisfied, I turned back to my story. Now I would have two things to show Gideon. When he saw the kind of pictures I took with my new camera, he'd realize what an asset I could be to him on an expedition. Meanwhile, I'd have to finish my story, so I could show him that, too.

Then a horrid thought struck me. I didn't know how long Gideon was going to stay. Suppose he found a house he liked, bought it, and then went away? My heart sank. The prospect of life without Gideon seemed colorless and dead. I had to work fast so that he would remember me and would always want to come back to Peabody after his travels in order to see me. I made a mental note to ask him how long he planned to stay, and looked down again at the words I had written. The conductor was still shouting. I would have to look that up in a French dictionary when I got a chance. In the meantime I finished the sentence so I could go on. "A little conductor with a mustache shouted, 'All aboard,' in French."

Chapter 4

Gideon was sitting alone in the living room when I came downstairs that night, and like the perfect gentleman he is, he stood up as I entered the room. I paused for a moment with his broad smile upon me, not knowing exactly what to do, but he soon put me at my ease.

"You look very pretty," he said. "I'm sure you'll put all the other women here tonight to shame."

He had called me a woman!

"Oh, wait till you see Mother," I said, passing off the compliment easily. I perched myself on the hassock and he sat down again.

"Who's coming tonight?" he asked.

"Just the Lindens and Julie and her cousin."

"Sounds fascinating."

"No, it isn't. Mrs. Linden and Julie Fanelle are Mother's best friends. Mr. Linden is a big shot down at the bank. I don't know anything about Julie's cousin, except that he's a college boy and that Julie and Mother thought it would be sweet if I met him. Big deal."

"So naturally," Gideon said, "you have started out with a prejudice against Julie's poor cousin even before you've met him. Am I right?"

"Yes," I said. "Do you like having people pushed on you?"

"Certainly not." And then he grinned and said softly, "And I suppose Julie is an attractive spinster who is supposed to make the evening more interesting for me."

A giggle escaped me. "How did you guess?"

"That is always happening to me," he said. "Anyway, tell me about her."

Temptation rose up wickedly within me. This was my chance. If I could poke fun at Julie, maybe I could make her seem ridiculous in Gideon's eyes. If we could laugh at her together, it would be something between us—a secret, something to glance at each other about across the room.

But Gideon was looking at me curiously. "What's she like?" he asked.

And then I thought about her, really thought about Julie, my old friend. When I was younger she used to come over and stay with me when Mother and Daddy went away on trips, and we used to have lovely times together on those week ends. They were so much fun that I hated them to end and longed to go home with her afterward. She never forgot my birthday or Christmas, and when I had problems I could take them to her and talk them over even more easily than with my own mother. In the library, she would always wink at me over the lending desk and glance at my books, as she had Saturday, to see what I was reading. I could never get anything past her.

It was silly for me now to be jealous of her when she hadn't even met Gideon yet. After all, it wasn't her fault that Mother wanted to couple her with him.

A nice warm feeling came over me at the thought of Julie. It felt so much better to love her again instead of hating her, the way I had for a while last night.

"She must be very wonderful," said Gideon, "to make you smile like that."

"Oh, she is, she really is. Julie's just about the best person in the world. And I don't think I have a better friend anywhere. Mother says she's been the best influence for the good in my whole life."

"Sort of a Sunday-school teacher type," said Gideon, and he winced a little.

"No, she isn't stuffy at all! Good things should be bright and gay and fresh, and that's the way Julie is."

"I see," he said. "She must be pretty then."

"Not exactly. You don't even think of that. She's small and fair and sort of well filled out—but not plump at all really. I guess you'd say she's the kind of person who grows on you. You'll see."

"Well, I hope I'm around long enough for her to grow on me then."

"When are you going to leave, Gideon?" I asked, finally calling him by his first name, because it seemed so natural. "I hope you're going to be around for a while."

"So do I. If I find a house I'd like to spend the rest of the summer here before I wander off again."

"Did you see anything you liked today?"

"Yes, as a matter of fact. But I want to take one more look at it tomorrow before I make up my mind."

Just then the doorbell rang, and I heard Julie's laugh on the front porch. She was opening the door as I ran into the hall.

"Mother," I yelled up the stairs, "Julie's here."

"Tell her I'll be right down!" Mother called. "You make the introduction, Christy."

I think now that Mother stayed upstairs on purpose so Gideon wouldn't see through her little scheme. With me introducing them, it made it all seem sort of innocent somehow.

Introductions always seem horrible to me. Everyone

talks at once, and it's hard to get things straight, and nobody seems to know quite what to say. At the same time Julie was introducing her cousin Frank to me, I was introducing Gideon to her, and for a minute everyone shouted at everyone else and then we just stood there in silence. I saw Julie's hand disappear in Gideon's big one and heard her mumble something about his books being very popular in the library, and he gave her that urbane smile of his and the little half bow.

I felt a measure of satisfaction. There didn't seem to be much to worry about. Then I turned to Frank and saw a gangling boy close to six feet tall who looked as though he had never eaten much since he was born. He was dark, with a lot of hair that needed cutting and heavy beetle brows that gave him a perpetual scowl— or maybe a worried look is a better description. His brown eyes were hidden slightly behind a pair of glasses.

"Hi, Frank," I said.

"Hi," he growled, and gave me a kind of accusing look.

There was a profound silence among the four of us for a moment. I wished Mother would come down and take over, but since I was the hostess—temporarily—I had to do something.

"Let's all go into the living room," was the only remark I could think of.

"Yes, let's," said Gideon, and I looked at him quickly,

thinking he was being sarcastic, but his eyes were twin-kling. He was aware of the silly awkwardness of the situation. Well, I guess the others were too, except that no one else felt amused.

Then Julie helped me out. "Did you read that book last night, Christy?" she asked.

"It kept me up half the night."

"Well, you weren't alone. I took one home too, and even Emma sneaked one out when she thought I wasn't looking." She smiled politely at Gideon. "I guess there's going to be a rash of people reading your books now that you're in town, Mr. Myles."

"Is that so?" he said. "But I thought you told me my books were very popular."

Julie refused to be flustered at that. She laughed. "You know perfectly well what I mean. People like Christy who ordinarily never read them are going to be curious."

"But you read one last night too, and my old friend Emma . . . Morrison, isn't it? Are you insinuating that intelligent people don't read them as a usual thing?"

"Well," Julie said slowly, "if you want my honest opinion—"

"I do," he said, baiting her.

"You write with great facility, and you have a narra-tive style that is very effective."

"Come again?" said Gideon.

"In other words, your books are popular, but they'll never set the world on fire."

Julie said it all without a blush. She believed what she said, and she wasn't going to butter him up in the least. I admired her courage but wondered at her foolishness. Didn't she know men liked to be flattered? Even I knew that. No wonder she had never married; men *were* scared of her, as Daddy said. Not that Gideon looked scared. He had his finger on the side of his nose and was smiling a little.

At that moment Mother and Daddy came into the room.

"Well," Mother said explosively, "how's everyone getting along? Do you all know each other? I'm sorry I wasn't here to meet you at the door, Julie. I suppose this is Frank. How do you do, Frank? I hope you're going to like living in Peabody."

Frank got to his feet with his arms dangling at his sides. When Mother came over to him, he extended one of them.

"Yes, I do," he muttered inanely, and then as she moved away, he collapsed again into the deep recesses of Daddy's old leather chair.

"Your friend has just been telling me that she doesn't like my books," Gideon told Mother.

Mother's face fell a mile.

"I didn't say that *exactly*," Julie said steadfastly.

"She's right anyway," said Gideon. "I'm a competent hack. And no one knows that better than I do. Still, it pays awfully well, and I enjoy my life. Do you enjoy yours, Miss Fanelle?"

This time Julie did have the grace to blush. "In an unspectacular way, I suppose," she said.

The atmosphere was tense all of a sudden. What had been a sort of teasing byplay for a while had suddenly become serious. It was an uncomfortable situation, but at the same time I felt a delicious sense of relief. Why, they didn't like each other at all! In spite of his teasing, it was possible that Gideon was peeved deep down at her superior attitude over his writing. And Julie—why had she been so insultingly honest? Perhaps she couldn't help herself. It was her way with men. She felt unsure with them, and her only defense was to pretend she was just as smart as they were. But she had really put her foot in it this time. I felt sorry for her.

Mother tried to say something to change the subject, but fortunately, the Lindens arrived then, and the air cleared a bit as more introductions took place. Everyone talked at once again, and I noticed that Gideon had gradually drifted over to Julie. He sat on the arm of her chair, and they seemed to be continuing their argument. Julie's face was flushed and I could see that she really wasn't enjoying herself much. Gideon acted perfectly at ease, and the smile remained on his face. It was impossible to tell whether he was angry or not, but I suspected that if he ever was angry he would behave just as he did now, hiding it under a calm veneer and in quiet, almost cryptic sarcasm.

Then, curiously, I glanced over at Frank. He had found one of Daddy's science-fiction magazines and was deeply immersed in it, sitting low on his spine with his chin resting on his chest. Mother had placed a dish of peanuts on the table beside him, and occasionally, without looking up, he reached out a great paw, scooped up about half a pound of them, and absently ate them out of his hand.

I walked over to him. "Do you always read at people's houses?" I asked.

"Only when I have to go to them," he said, his face still in the book.

"Didn't you want to come tonight?"

"No," he said. He went on reading, and I looked at him helplessly for a minute, then shrugged my shoulders and walked away.

Mother caught me at the doorway as I tried to sneak upstairs. "Where do you think you're going? You have a guest." She nodded her head toward Frank.

"He's reading."

"Of course he is. The poor boy hasn't anyone to talk to."

"Mother, he told me he'd *rather* read. He doesn't like social occasions."

She fixed me with a beady stare for a minute and then said in her voice-that-will-brook-no-nonsense, "You will go right in there and ask him to go downstairs and play ping-pong."

"What if he doesn't want to play ping-pong?"

"He will. All boys like activity. Really, Christy, I don't know what's come over you lately."

She gave me one last glare and then went back to her guests, flashing a hostess smile. Sighing, I went back to Frank. He didn't look to me like a boy who liked activity. Just the same, I snatched the book from his grasp and took his hand.

"Come on," I said.

"Where?"

"Mother says we *have* to play ping-pong."

I tried to pull him up, but he was a dead weight. Then he looked over at Mother, and seeing her eyes upon us, he said, "Oh, all right."

We call the room in the basement the Club Cellar, but that is a loose word for it. Daddy is always talking about putting down asphalt tile, but he never gets around to it. All our old furniture is down there, including a drab gray couch, with the springs coming out of it. There is an old phonograph, but it won't play anything but 78 r.p.m. records, and even they sound pretty wheezy on it. When Frank and I got down there, we found some unwashed laundry on the ping-pong table, and I quickly threw it into the clothes hamper, hoping he hadn't noticed. I remembered hearing Mother ask Daddy to take the sheets down for her when she changed the beds yesterday. Apparently he had tossed them there and then something had interrupted him. I found the ping-pong paddles in the drawer in Mother's old kitchen cabinet and slid one across the table to Frank.

He took it listlessly. "You serve," he said.

We played in silence for a while. Neither one of us was any challenge for the other, and the ball clock-clocked hollowly back and forth for several minutes without either one of us missing it.

Finally Frank caught it in his hand. "Look," he said, "if we have to play this, at least let's put a little life into it."

"O.K.," I said.

He served hard and the ball smacked into the net. Reaching across easily he picked it up without comment and tried again. This time it went over and I hit it back to him. He returned it without effort and tried to put it where I couldn't reach it. But I did. We were both trying hard, but we were evenly matched. Across the table I could see little beads of perspiration on

Frank's forehead. Then he caught the ball again and put down his paddle.

"Can I take off my coat?" he asked.

"Of course." I watched him for a second and then said, "Would you like a Coke?"

"Yes, I would."

I started up the steps and he followed. "I'll help you," he said.

We got four Cokes out of the refrigerator, and I made us some sandwiches—with Frank's help (he spread the mayonnaise and put on the lettuce)—and then, armed with these, plus a box of cookies, we went down to the Club Cellar again.

We put the whole mess on the ping-pong table and dragged it over to the old couch and sat there gorging ourselves.

"I like to see a girl eat," he said, between bites. "Most girls make me feel like a glutton, they're so picky."

"Oh, I love to eat," I told him truthfully, "but I didn't think you would. If I ate like this all the time, I'd be a barrel, but you're so nice and sk—slim."

"It's nervous tension," he said seriously. "I'm very nervous, and I walk a lot. I'm not very athletic, but I am a good walker. Not many people are good walkers, you know."

"No, I guess they aren't. Why, take Daddy, for instance. He gets in the car to mail a letter. That's why he's getting tubby."

"Exactly," said Frank, with profound conviction. "Now, when I get to be your father's age, I'll look the same as I do now. Of course, my life's work will help— and I'm not afraid of hard work, not when it's something I like."

"I'll bet you're going to be a scientist. That's why you like to read science fiction."

"It isn't quite like that," he said. "But the work I want to do does take a good thoughtful mind and a lot of figuring. It combines careful analysis, a great deal of detective work, and a knowledge of the past."

"Well, it sounds fascinating," I told him politely, "but I still don't know what you're talking about. What is it you want to be?"

"Didn't Julie tell you? I'm going to be an archaeologist."

I felt deflated. I had a vague idea of what an archaeologist was, but I wasn't sure. It seemed to be connected in my mind with old movies on television where Boris Karloff or somebody digs up a mummy that comes to life and kills people.

"You mean," I asked, "Egyptian tombs and things like that?"

Frank smiled condescendingly. It was the first time

I had seen him smile, and it made him look almost pleasant.

"Well, partly," he said in a patronizing way. "I guess that's what the average person thinks of first, but there is much more to it than that."

"Tell me," I said meekly.

"Well, did you know, for instance, that before Schliemann dug up Troy, people didn't even believe it had ever existed?"

"No, I didn't," I said, and that was no lie.

"All his life he read and reread Homer, and he was convinced that Troy was in Turkey, so he went there with his wife—who was Greek, by the way—and started digging."

"That must have been fun for her—his wife, I mean."

But my sarcasm was lost on Frank. "Oh, yes, she was a perfect partner for him. Anyhow, he dug right through Troy—missed it entirely."

"That's too bad," I said, wondering what the point of the story was.

"No, you don't understand. He may not have recognized Troy, but that doesn't minimize the importance of his discovery. *He* started it, you see!"

Frank's eyes were bright, and he had forgotten to eat his sandwich. He waved it around in the air. "And Pompeii!" he said. "That was another one. Buried for centuries under lava and ash and perfectly preserved just as it was the day it ended. Because of archaeology, we can walk through those streets now, like going back in time. They've made casts of the bodies so that today we can see them just as they were in their death agony."

"How horrible," I breathed, intrigued in spite of myself.

Frank looked at me for a minute as though he had just seen me. Then he took a thoughtful bite out of his sandwich. "Yes, it is horrible if you want to look at it like that. But the real interest is in the history and in finding these things that have been handled and used by people long dead and forgotten. Do you realize how our knowledge of history can be broadened by such discoveries?"

"I never thought of it before, but it's true," I said sincerely.

Again Frank looked at me. I felt embarrassed under his scrutiny.

"You're a very understanding girl," he said. "I don't talk about this to many people."

"I'm flattered that you wanted to talk about it to me, then."

"Well," he said slowly, "at first I had some doubts about you. I thought you were like most girls. They think I'm a bore."

"Oh, no!" I protested, but I squirmed guiltily.

Frank stared into space, looking solemn and sipping

his Coke. "Do you want to play any more ping-pong?" he asked.

"No. Do you?"

"No."

We sat there quietly for a while, not saying anything, and it came over me that I was very comfortable with Frank. But I hoped he had exhausted the subject of digging and ancient history for the evening.

We could hear them talking over our heads. For only six people, they were making a terrific din.

"I hate parties," Frank said, nodding his head toward the ceiling.

"This isn't a party. It's just a get-together of a few people."

"It sounds like a party."

We listened like two conspirators, but it was impossible to make out any one voice. I wondered what Gideon was doing and if he had noticed that I was gone. I hoped he had.

"Do you like social functions and all that stupidity?" Frank asked suddenly.

"Sometimes. I like gaiety and fun and dancing."

"I suppose you would. You're still very young."

"So are you."

He glowered at me. "I feel older than most people," he said.

We had finished up the sandwiches, the Cokes, and

the box of cookies. "Would you like anything else?" I asked.

Frank picked up a crumb out of the empty box with the tips of two fingers. "Just a Coke, I guess."

I went up for two more Cokes, and when I got back I saw that Frank had taken out a pipe and a tobacco pouch. Both of them looked very new. He started stuffing tobacco into the pipe.

"I see you smoke a pipe," I said unnecessarily.

"Um," said Frank. He had put the stem between his teeth and was laboriously trying to light his pipe.

"I like to see a man smoke a pipe," I said.

Frank gave me a stiff sidewise smile. Then the tobacco caught the match flame and a glow of satisfaction spread over his countenance, but he carefully replaced it with his usual serious expression.

"So do I," he said. "I think you'll find that more thinkers smoke pipes than cigarettes. There's something about the business of having to fill a pipe that leads to more sober thought. A pipe smoker is usually a mature man who never does anything haphazardly or on the spur of the moment."

I could believe that of Frank. He sat back puffing like a chimney and gazing across at the washing machine.

"I haven't decided yet," he announced pontifically, "what branch of archaeology appeals to me the most.

There's still a great deal to be discovered in South America."

"Oh?" I said, wriggling. Archaeology could be interesting in small doses, but I didn't feel much like going into it again. The old overstuffed sofa was soft and warm, and Frank's arm, which was lazily lying on the back of it, was pressing my hair against the back of my neck. It felt hot and sticky. Upstairs I heard Gideon's laugh ring out, and my heart turned over with longing. I was being left out of everything. Mother had certainly gotten rid of "the kids" in a very underhanded manner.

Nervously I got up and went over to the door and looked up into the back yard, where fireflies were flickering against the trees. Frank had stopped talking, and as I turned back I saw him looking at me in a questioning way. Suddenly I was very sorry for him. I felt that his seriousness, while real, hid a lack of confidence in himself where girls were concerned. He feared being a bore, but he couldn't seem to avoid being one.

I smiled. "It's awfully hot, isn't it?" I said.

"Yes," he said, looking uncertain, but as I continued to smile, he smiled back. He didn't look half so odd when he smiled.

"Would you like to play some more ping-pong," he asked.

"No. You asked me that once. I think we've found

out we don't do that very well." Upstairs Gideon
laughed again. Restlessness overcame me. I *had* to see
what was happening. "If you don't mind," I said, "I'm
going to go upstairs for just a minute. I think I've probably eaten off all my lipstick."

"You look fine," Frank said.

"Just the same," I said, edging toward the stairs, "I
think I'd better. I'll be right back."

Without stopping at the living room I ran upstairs
and added the lipstick and combed my hair back. All
the curl was gone so I tied it up, and it felt cooler. The
pony tail did look babyish, though. Maybe Mother was
right.

Downstairs again, I stopped at the living-room door.
No one saw me for a while, so I had a chance to ob-
serve. Gideon was sitting on the arm of Julie's chair.
As I watched, he leaned over her and said something.
She flushed and laughed, tilting her head back to look
up at him. He smiled and looked away from her, almost
exultantly. It was then that he saw me.

"Why, Christy!" He got up and came over to me.
"Where have you been all this time?"

"Downstairs with Frank. Mother wanted us to play
ping-pong."

"And did you?"

"We were dutiful and tried, but it was deadly. How
do you like Julie?" I whispered.

"She's a good sport. We've been badgering each other all evening, but I think she enjoys it." He looked over at her and grinned, and a jealous pang shot through me.

"I'm glad you like her," I lied.

Just then Frank came up behind me. "Would you like to stay up here for a while?" he asked.

I looked from Julie back to Gideon and managed a smile. "I don't think so," I said. "Why don't we go out on the porch? It's cooler out there."

Still puffing on his pipe, he followed me out. I felt trapped, and although I did like him, I couldn't help wishing he would go away. I had had a chance to look at the clock. It was only ten, and I was sure no one would go home before midnight. Covering a sigh, I smiled at Frank. "Tell me more about archaeology," I said sweetly.

Chapter 5

Daddy and Gideon went out early in the morning to take another look at the house Gideon was interested in, and while they were gone I went downtown to buy my camera. I was lucky enough to find a sale on cameras, so I had three dollars left over after I had bought one and some film, and I was feeling pretty good as I walked along Main Street on my way home. The first thing I wanted to do, I decided, was to take a picture of Gideon—without being too obvious about it, of course.

I was passing Pierre's Beauty Salon when the great idea struck me. I would get my hair cut! It would make me look a lot older to have short hair instead of that pony tail hanging down my back. Mother wouldn't mind my using the left-over money for that; she would be pleased. I hesitated only a moment before I pushed open the door and entered the air-conditioned interior. Pierre was sitting at the desk where they take appointments. His name isn't really Pierre—it's Pat O'Grady and he's from Brooklyn, New York—but that plainly doesn't suit his calling.

"Why, Christy Collier," he said looking up. "How are you? Does your mother want an appointment?"

"No," I said firmly. "I do."

He lifted his eyebrows and stared at me. "A permanent? For that I think some of your hair would have to go."

"All of it has to go—well, not all—you know what I mean. And I don't want a permanent. I just want it cut—nice and short and sophisticated." I looked at him imploringly. "Do you have time to do it now, please, while I still have the nerve?"

Pierre lifted one shoulder and gestured at the empty shop. "Do I have the time? What do you think? My first appointment isn't for a half hour yet." He led me into one of the booths and motioned for me to sit in the chair. "Come on. We'll make you beautiful."

I gripped the arms of the chair and shut my eyes. Suddenly I wondered if I was doing the right thing, and then I heard a noise near my ear. Snip! I opened my eyes. I could see Pierre in the mirror, standing there with a long strand of hair in his hand. It looked like limp straw, defenseless and lost.

"Oh, no!" I wailed. "I shouldn't have let you do it! Let me see. Is it too late?" I squirmed around in the seat. He had hacked it off about an inch below my ear.

"You did say you wanted it short," he pointed out kindly.

"Oh, but I don't think I'm going to like it!"

Pierre patted my shoulder. "It's natural for you to feel that way at first. Everyone does."

"Do they?"

"Of course. And besides, it's too late now. It's better to get it over with now, Christy. You'll like it when it's finished."

I shut my eyes again. "Tell me when it's over."

But I couldn't wait. I heard him cutting all around my head and then I looked again. My beautiful hair that had taken so many years to grow was lying on the floor like something that had been cast away as useless, and as for me—I looked *awful!* Not at all sophisticated and cute, but like a pathetic shorn lamb.

I clutched my head through the white cover that was draped over me. "What have you done to me?" I cried.

"I'm not finished yet, Christy," he said patiently. "It has to be shaped."

I looked into his eyes for reassurance and he smiled

encouragingly. Removing my hands, I looked again. I sighed.

"It needs something," I said in resignation. "Maybe it's still too long—that's it. It's too in-between-looking this way—like a child. All I need is a big hair ribbon. Cut it *really* short."

"Are you sure?"

"Yes, yes," I told him frantically. "I want it really short. Remember Mary Martin in *Peter Pan?*"

"But your hair is straight," he said.

"I don't care. The damage is done now. Cut away, Pierre."

"Your mother will kill me," he said.

I didn't meet anyone on the way home—probably because I took back streets. Fortunately, Daddy's car was still missing as I sneaked into the house. Mother was in the kitchen; I could hear her humming. I stood in the hall not knowing what to do. I longed for an unbiased opinion, and I knew Mother would give it to me, but I dreaded it. Still humming, she came out of the kitchen carrying a vase of fresh flowers.

Then she caught sight of me and gave a faint scream. In her hands the vase tottered precariously for a second. "Christy," she whispered, "what have you done?"

"I guess you can see what I've done."

"Your beautiful long hair!"

"But you didn't like it," I protested. "You were always complaining about it."

"I know I was, but—this! Come into the light where I can get a better look at you. Oh, Christy, Christy."

She went into the living room and put the flowers down and drew me over to the window. She looked for a long time, turning me around and touching my head wistfully. I wanted to cry. I knew I looked horrible, and I knew Gideon would think I looked horrible too.

"I'm sorry," I whimpered. "I just wanted to look grown-up. I'm tired of looking like a baby."

"Oh, darling," Mother said. She drew me to her. There were tears in her voice. Her body shook. And then I realized that she wasn't crying but laughing, almost hysterically.

"What's so funny?" I said loudly.

Her laughter became quite uncontrolled. Helplessly she sat down and wiped her eyes. "Forgive me, honey. It's cruel to laugh. But did you have to go to such lengths to age yourself?"

"I wish I was dead," I said fervently.

"Oh no you don't. Now don't be silly. Actually, you look quite cute. It'll take some getting used to, but when I do, I think I'm going to like it."

"You *think!*"

"Anyway, it will grow out and that's a comfort."

"Not for me!" I howled. "I hope Gid—other people won't laugh at me."

"I'll prepare them for it," she promised. There was the sound of Daddy's car pulling up outside. "There they are now," she said, giving me a gentle shove. "Get out of sight so I can tell them."

I pulled myself together and ran up the stairs. "I'm going to take a shower. There's hair down my back, and it itches."

However, once I was in the bathroom I stuck my head out of the door and listened.

"Gideon wants to buy the house," I heard Daddy say.

"Oh, wonderful. I'm so glad, Gideon," Mother said.

"We're going into the office and take care of the papers," said Daddy. "I have to call Jameson and tell him we've sold it. He might want to come over."

"Before you do that, there's something I want to tell you."

"What's the matter?" Daddy sounded worried.

"Nothing startling," Mother said soothingly. "It's just that Christy got her hair cut this morning."

"That's nice."

"She got it cut *very* short. I wanted to warn you. Don't laugh at her, Ralph. It's quite a shock when you first see her."

"What'd she do that for?"

"I think I know, but I'm not sure."

"Yes?" Daddy's voice sounded only half-interested. There was a pause.

"It's nothing," said Mother carefully. "Just tell her she looks nice, no matter what you think."

"All right," he said impatiently. "I've got more important things to think about right now."

I closed the bathroom door and leaned against it. I was trembling. Mother thought I looked terrible, and I did look terrible. I was an absolute mess. And not only that, she suspected something. What was it she knew—or thought she knew—but wouldn't tell? It was about Gideon, I was sure. It was sickening to think of her pitying me, condescending to me because of what she would think was only a crush. I looked in the mirror. There, are you satisfied? I said to myself. You've not only made yourself look like a boy, but you've made an ass of yourself, too. If you'd let yourself alone, no one would have known anything.

After my shower, without waiting for her to call me, I got Margo on the upstairs phone and told her I was coming over so we could bike out to the lake. I didn't feel like facing Gideon just yet.

Margo's jaw dropped when she saw me and she didn't say anything for a minute.

"Well," I said uncomfortably, "get it over with. I know I look like an idiot."

"Oh, no," she breathed. "Oh, Christy, I think it's *marvelous*. You have no idea what it does for you. I've been wanting to tell you for a long time that you ought to do something about your hair. It looked so ordinary, but I never dreamed you'd have nerve enough to go this far."

"My mother laughed when she saw me—actually laughed."

Margo shrugged her shoulders. "Well, *c'est la vie!* You know how parents are. If they don't suggest something themselves, they think it's no good. It's chick, I tell you, *très* chick."

Good old Margo. She made me feel so much better. And there is no flattery like imitation. She ran a hand over her own short hair. "I wonder," she said musingly. "No, I guess not. For me, it's short enough. I haven't a face like yours—I'd just look funny with my hair cropped any more than it is. But for you it's perfect."

I felt so much better now that I began to get hungry, so Margo suggested making sandwiches to take with us.

Later, at the lake, after a good invigorating swim, we ate them. As I lay in the sun, my hair dried quickly. There was a practical side to it, anyhow.

Margo turned over on her stomach and stretched like a cat. She looked pleased with herself about something. "Guess what?" she said triumphantly. "Steve called me last night and asked me if I could go with him to the

Elks' Dance on Labor Day, and Mother says I can go this year."

"The Elks' Dance?" I hadn't given it a thought. Up to now I had always been considered too young.

"We're sixteen," said Margo.

"I ought to be allowed to go," I said. "Daddy's on the committee, but he's never mentioned it to me. If you're going, though. . . ."

"I do wish you'd been nicer to Barry. He might have asked you."

"I wouldn't go if he did."

Margo sat up. "What's the matter with Barry, for heaven's sake?"

"Nothing. He's perfectly all right. Only, I . . . well. . . ." I pulled at a hayseed and started chewing on it for something to do.

Margo moved over and looked into my face shrewdly. "There's something fishy about you," she said, "and it seems to have started Saturday when that author arrived in town. You haven't got a crush on him by any chance, have you?"

"Don't be silly."

She slapped her knee. "I *knew* it! You're just the kind of impressionable girl who would go and do a thing like that."

"My goodness," I said airily, "you certainly sound like old Aunt Matilda all of a sudden."

"I may not have met him, but I *saw* him, and he's just the kind of person you'd go for. Handsome and rugged and sophisticated and just *darling*. But he's old enough to be your father."

"Not quite," I said, chewing the hayseed disdainfully.

"Then you do have a crush on him, don't you?"

I hated that word *crush*. I despised it. "I admire him very much," I said, "and I think he likes me. We have a lot in common."

Margo guffawed, but then she suddenly stopped herself and looked serious. "I'm sorry. I guess I'm being nasty. Maybe I'm even a little bit jealous. He *is* a dreamboat, and I don't blame you at all."

With that off her chest she flopped down on her stomach again, and there was a long silence between us. The sun on our backs was tempered by a breeze that whipped through the grasses and made little whitecaps on the lake. I struggled with conflicting emotions. My precious secret was a secret no longer. My mother knew and now Margo did, too. I was sorry for that, but since it had happened I found I wanted to talk about it. Slowly, and then in a rush, the words began pouring out of me. I told her how I felt, about how wonderful he was and about my jealousy of Julie. It felt good to talk about it with somebody. Margo nodded her head sagely as she listened.

"Of course, you know this is between the two of us,"

I finished. "You must never betray me in word or deed."

"Have I ever?" she asked.

"No," I said.

"I feel sorry for you, though," she added. "You might as well face it—you haven't got a chance. He'll just think of you as a child—it's inevitable—and you'll have Julie working against you, too."

Yes, there was always Julie.

As Margo and I biked back to town I had two important thoughts in my mind. One, I was going to go to the Elks' Dance too, and getting that permission was the first thing to accomplish. Second, somehow or other I had to arrange for Gideon to take me. Of course, I couldn't ask him—the very thought of such a thing filled me with terror—but perhaps, with the aid of a few subtle hints, I could get him to ask me.

I had forgotten all about my hair as I rode up to the house, propped my bike against the porch and bearded the lion in his den. Daddy was sitting at his desk. He looked up at me and said coolly, "I see you got your hair cut."

I shrugged off his remark. Margo had given me confidence, and what *he* thought didn't matter.

"Yes," I said, and then went on to more important matters. "Margo's parents are letting her go to the Elks'

Dance this year. She already has a date for it and everything. I want to go too, Daddy. After all, I am sixteen."

"I'm well aware of it," he said. "I suppose you've already accepted a date for it, so what I think doesn't matter."

"How can I accept a date if I don't know if I'm going?"

"I'm sure you wouldn't let that stop you. But. . . . Yes, I guess you can go—if it's all right with your mother."

"Oh, I'm sure it would be. Thanks, Daddy."

I quickly got Mother's consent and drew a sigh of relief, although it really wasn't necessary. I had been pretty sure they'd agree to it.

Gideon had gone out somewhere, but he came home near dinnertime as I was setting the table.

He came into the dining room and grinned delightedly at me. "Hello, Peter Pan," he said.

I wanted to kiss him.

Chapter 6

Julie came over that night to do some typing for Daddy. I don't know whether he had called her or not, but there she was. I was finding it more and more difficult to continue liking my old friend. Whether it was an act or not, though, she did shut herself away in the office for a time, and I heard the typewriter clicking away. Once Gideon went in and sat on the desk and started talking to her, and I heard her say, "Not now. I'm busy. I'll talk to you later," and he came out of there meekly. She was apparently playing hard to get.

I got out my new camera and went in and took a picture of her at work, and this started a conversation with Gideon about photography, so I went upstairs and came down with my old pictures for him to see.

He looked them over carefully. "You know," he said, "I think you have a knack. You seem to know the exact moment to snap a picture. And the composition is perfect. This one of the blue jay is a small masterpiece."

"I have thought of making a career of it," I said.

"You could do worse," he agreed. "Let me see that picture of Julie when it's developed."

I promised I would. Gideon turned to Mother and started talking about something else, and once, in the middle of a typical exaggerated gesture as he told of his adventures, I snapped a picture of him.

He looked at me in surprise. "That was sneaky of you."

"If this turns out well," I said, "I'll call it 'Gideon Myles in Action.'"

"I'm afraid you've got me pegged," he said wryly. "You're getting as bad as Julie."

"Did I hear my name mentioned?" asked Julie, coming out of the office.

"Your friend Christy is getting as insulting as you are," he said.

"Good," said Julie.

And then she started talking about his new house. Julie said she guessed that that meant his stay would be extended, and Gideon admitted that it would. Julie asked him when he was going to move in, and he said he had to buy some furniture first, and as soon as it could be delivered, he would move in.

"I'm going shopping tomorrow," he added.

It was then that Julie had the idea of making a party out of cleaning up his house. Her father had a small pickup truck and could get the furniture for Gideon and deliver it to the house on the Fourth of July. We could all turn out en masse, clean the house together, and move the furniture in. With everyone helping, she said, the job would be done in no time, and we could finish the day with a swim in the lake and a picnic on the beach.

Everyone agreed that this was a wonderful idea. I did too, only it meant I had just a few days to get Gideon to ask me to go to the dance.

The next morning a wonderful opportunity presented itself. Gideon looked at me across the breakfast table and suddenly said, "Say, Christy, how about coming to town with me today and helping me shop for furniture?"

I paused with a piece of toast halfway to my mouth. This was too good to be true. Then I looked at Mother, and for a minute she looked as if she was going to say, "Christy doesn't know anything about selecting furniture," but she didn't say it. Instead, she smiled at me and said, "That'll be fun for her, Gideon. Thanks for asking her."

An hour later I was sitting with him in the front seat of his car with the top down and the air blowing through my cropped hair. Everyone looked at us as we drove downtown. I felt terribly important, but I managed to act casual.

Actually Gideon didn't need me along at all. He had his own ideas about what he wanted, and ordered most of the stuff at the Army Surplus Store—bunk beds and army blankets and camping equipment. For a while I thought he would never leave, because he got into a spirited conversation about fishing, with the owner of the store, and I spent a dreary time staring at old guns and uniforms and army things covered with dust. Finally, though, he remembered I was there, and we went to a secondhand store for things like a table and chairs and a stove and a refrigerator. He did let me pick out the curtains later in Lane's Department Store, and I chose dark green burlap, which seemed masculine enough. Besides, I thought they would make the house look underwatery and mysterious, with the sun shining through them. We also picked bedspreads of the same color, and sheets and tablecloths and dishes and cooking equipment. That part of it was fun, and I tried to imagine that we were engaged to be married and that we were buying things for our home. A gray-and-green hooked rug from an antique store and a matted one for the bedroom completed the shopping.

Gideon stood in the sun outside the antique store and squinted down at me. "Well, Christy, you've added the feminine touch to my house. Thanks for the help."

"I enjoyed it," I said. "I can't wait to see the results."

"Now for some lunch. How about it?"

"Sure," I said.

He took me over to the hotel, where they have a big airy dining room with French windows looking out over the square, and clean white tablecloths, and a man who plays the organ. I felt positively regal walking in there with Gideon, who pulled out my chair for me.

A waitress came over. She was a pretty but slightly tired-looking girl with suspiciously blond hair. Her eyes lit up when she saw Gideon. "Oh, it's you," she said. "We've been wondering why we haven't seen you lately."

"Been staying with friends," Gideon told her.

"Oh? Well, that's always better than a hotel. You know, I was telling my boy friend about your experiences on the raft in the Pacific; he said he never heard such a tall tale in his life, but I told him he should have heard *you* tell it."

Gideon laughed. "Stories always lose something when you hear them secondhand."

"It was true, wasn't it?"

"Every word," Gideon said. His eyes were twinkling.

"Aw, go on! You've been pulling my leg." The girl laughed too, and I could see it didn't matter if he had fooled her—she liked him too much. She took our orders and went away.

"Everywhere you go you make friends, don't you?" I said.

"I told you," said Gideon, "I like people."

"And they like you." Then I looked at him doubtfully. "Was it true?"

"What?"

"That story you told her."

"Why, Christy, do you suspect me too?"

"I don't know," I mused. It was beginning to occur to me that a lot of Gideon's stories might be as fictional as his books. He was like a little boy daring people to believe all his tall tales. For a minute I felt almost motherly.

But Gideon had been watching me closely. "Surely you're not going to believe that waitress. She's used to traveling salesmen. They love to spin yarns."

"That means she knows the type when she sees it."

Gideon hung his head. "Alas," he said, "I've been exposed. Now you know what a fraud I am."

"Gideon Myles," I said, "you're just impossible."

He laughed and reached over and patted my hand. "Don't give me away, will you?"

"Darn you! I'm probably the only person in town who believed everything you told us." I was carrying the joke along, but secretly a twinge of disappointment stabbed at me. Maybe he really never had been on any jungle expeditions either, and if not, my being a photographer wouldn't matter to him very much. But at least I had one consolation. There was still the story. I hadn't finished it yet, but then and there, I vowed I would that night.

"What's your favorite song, Christy?" he asked suddenly.

"Why?"

He nodded toward the organist, who had been softly playing all along. "I'll ask Will to play it for you."

"You mean he would?"

"Of course."

I thought quickly. What was my favorite song? Not that it mattered then. I wanted to pick out something that would always remind me of Gideon. Something significant, but I didn't know what. I looked at him helplessly. "I can't think of one right now," I said. "You ask him for one, something that you think I would like." That was a clever move, I thought. Now I would find out a little about what Gideon really thought of me.

I watched him cross the big, almost empty dining

room, masculine and sure of himself among the white tablecloths. He said something to Will, who smiled in my direction. He began to play as Gideon started back toward me, and I listened to the opening strains as he approached me. "Greensleeves." Listening to it, my heart seemed to stop—that is the only way I can describe the feeling I had. Although I never took my eyes from Gideon, I could see out of the corner of my eye the little puffed sleeve of my best off-the-shoulder summer dress, which I had worn for this occasion. Its color was a soft green.

The sweet old English tune filled the room as Gideon stood over me for a moment and then leaned down and whispered, "Did I choose all right?"

"Oh, Gideon, thank you," I said softly.

Then I listened to it without saying a word, and tried not to let my adoration show in my eyes when I looked at him.

During lunch I told Gideon about the Elks' Dance and how I was going to be allowed to go this year. "Now that you're sure to be here for a while, you'll be going too, won't you," I said carefully.

"I suppose so," he said, munching a roll. "It hadn't occurred to me."

"But you really ought to go. Everyone'll be expecting it. And all the girls will be hoping you'll ask them to go with you."

"Gad! What a horrible thought!"

"Why is it?"

"You conjure up a perfect picture of lonely females who are dying to get their claws into some man. Ask one of them to go to a dance in a town like this, and the next thing you know you're standing at the altar, watching her triumphant march toward you down the aisle."

"I think you're exaggerating very much," I said, quite piqued all of a sudden.

"Well, maybe not all of them," he said in a conciliatory way. "You, my dear, are different—or are you?" He cocked his head at me and lifted his eyebrows appraisingly.

"No, I'm not. I certainly hope I'll get married someday."

"Never fear, you will—but not, I hope, until after a wonderful few years as the town beauty. For sweet goodness' sake, Christy, don't get married right after high school the way so many silly kids do."

"Why are you so dead set against marriage?"

"I'm not really—for other people. I just don't want it for me. I enjoy life tremendously, you know, just as I am. And I hope you will too for a while."

"I suppose I will," I said, repressing a sigh. But at least there was one good thing about his not wanting to get married. That would save him for me. When I was older and more sophisticated, perhaps I could change his mind.

We finished our dinner and went outside. The sunlight was blinding after the dimness of the restaurant. When he got to the car, Gideon leaned against the door thoughtfully.

"Say, let's go over to the library and see Julie."

"Julie? Why? I thought you wanted to stay away from marriage-minded women." The words came out of me before I thought, and I immediately wished them unsaid.

"Dare I suspect you of being catty, Christy?" he asked jokingly.

"Certainly not," I said, but I was embarrassed.

"Actually, I think I ought to tell her where we got the furniture, so Mr. Fanelle can pick it up in his truck."

"Let's go then," I said, and got into the car.

Julie was at the return desk when we went into the library. There was no one there except one nearsighted old man who was reading a newspaper with a magnifying glass. Julie smiled when she saw us, and as Gideon leaned over the desk talking to her quietly, I wandered around the familiar place. Back among the fiction I accidentally came upon Frank, who was putting books back on the shelves from one of those carts they push around. He blushed when he saw me and stood there uncomfortably with both hands holding one book. I had forgotten he worked there, but of course I didn't let him know that.

"Hello, Frank," I said.

"Hi, Christy," he said, and he turned the book around in his hands.

"It sure is quiet in here today."

"Yes," he said. He looked down at the book and then put it away and picked up another one. "I wanted to tell you I had a good time at your house the other night," he said abruptly.

"I'm glad."

"I was thinking—if it was all right with you, I mean —that I might come over and see you again. Tonight maybe."

I thought of my story and shook my head. "Tonight there's something I have to do."

"Oh," said Frank.

He let the matter drop. Apparently the one request had taken all his nerve. I wondered idly if I ought to suggest the following night to him. Frankly, the idea of listening to him talk about archaeology again didn't appeal to me particularly.

Frank pushed the cart farther along the shelves, and I watched him hesitatingly. As he reached the end of the shelf a girl came around it and stopped when she saw him.

"Oh, there you are! Hello," she said.

It was Milly Baintree, a girl in my class at school. She isn't one of my close friends, although we have always been sort of friendly. She's a nice-enough-looking girl, but I always considered her personality a little flat. Frank seemed to know her already, though, and to like her. They talked to each other, and I moved away. At the other end of the room I saw Gideon still talking to Julie and laughing. They were always laughing at something, it seemed to me. I looked back at Milly and Frank. I suddenly felt very friendless and lost there, in the middle of these two absorbed couples, and although it seems petty, at that moment I began to hate Milly Baintree. Frank didn't interest me particularly, but still, I had met him first, and I rather considered him my property. I walked over to them again.

"Hi, Milly," I said.

"Oh, hello, Christy," she said, too sweetly.

"Do you two know each other?" asked Frank.

"Of course. We go to school together, silly," she said coyly.

"Frank," I said, "when you're through, I want to talk to you. O.K.?"

"Sure thing," he said.

I left them alone again, but I could see that Frank was trying to get rid of Milly now, and that made me feel better. But I wasn't very proud of myself. What was

the matter with me, anyway? I made my way to the
M's and picked out another book by Gideon to read,
and then Frank came back to me.

"What did you want to say?" he asked.

"I was going to suggest, before Milly interrupted us,
that you ought to come over tomorrow night instead of
tonight—that is, if you haven't made other plans."

"Other plans?" he said vaguely. "No, I. . . ." He
looked toward Milly, who was leaving the library, and
a light dawned in his eyes. "I haven't made any other
dates," he said. "I'd like very much to come over tomorrow. Around seven-thirty?"

"Yes," I said.

He seemed very pleased with himself all of a sudden,
and I realized that he thought I was jealous of Milly.
The very idea of his thinking such a thing made me boil
inside, but I managed to smile. And he smiled back at
me with renewed confidence in himself.

Then he looked at me judicially. "That's a pretty
dress you're wearing," he said.

"Thank you," I replied.

"But what did you do to your hair?"

"I had it cut. Don't you like it? Gideon says I look
like Peter Pan."

He stared at me and frowned. "Yes, I suppose so, but
I kind of liked it long."

He *would* say that!

"Well," I replied, in a huff, "I'm sorry you think it's ugly."

"I didn't say that. You *couldn't* be ugly, Christy."

In his anxious desire to make amends he took my hand, and then we both stared down at it in embarrassment. But he didn't let go. He forced himself to look at me. "I think you're the prettiest girl I ever saw," he said.

"You don't have to go that far," I said softly, but I was pleased.

We were alone among the books. Their different-colored backs were turned toward us all along the shelves. It was a wonderful place to kiss someone, and I could see that Frank was thinking of just that. It would have been fun, in a way; I had never been kissed in a public library. But just the same, I knew I didn't want him to do it. Not today, not after "Greensleeves." I turned away from him and pretended to be looking for a book, and the moment passed safely by. But it left me with a nice feeling. It is pleasant to know that a boy wants to kiss you, especially after he has just told you you are the prettiest girl in town.

Chapter 7

On Tuesday night I finished my story about the Orient Express, and Wednesday morning it had to be typed, though haltingly, so Gideon could read it. He was gone all day—out to his house, I suspected, which he was probably cleaning to save the rest of us the trouble on the Fourth, which was Friday. I had also heard him mention paint, so I supposed he would get that done too on Thursday. Time was running out for me. After Gideon moved I would probably seldom see him, and any chance of his asking me to the dance would be gone. He *knew* I could go, and yet he had made no more mention of it.

He came in just before supper and went upstairs to

take a shower. I heard the water running and later the sound of his footsteps going to his room. Since the library closed at six, Frank would no doubt arrive sometime around seven-thirty, as he had promised, so I didn't have much time. I picked up the story and tapped its ten pages neatly together on the desk. It was good; I was sure of it. Nevertheless, I felt breathless and weak in the knees as I ran up the stairs and knocked softly on the door to Gideon's room.

"Yes?" he called.

"It's me, Christy," I whispered. "I have something I'd like you to read—if you don't mind."

He opened the door. His hair was damp and uncombed and sticking up on his head. He grinned. "What is it?" he asked.

"A story."

"Who wrote it?" The grin faded and he looked resigned, instead.

"I'm afraid I did," I said, beginning to feel more qualms about it than ever. I looked down at the title page. "Death Rides the Orient Express," by Christine Collier. I had thought the typewritten words looked much more professional and impressive than they had in longhand, but now I wasn't so sure. As a matter of fact, I was no longer sure I wanted Gideon to read it. But it was too late, for he had taken it from me.

"I'll read it," he said suavely. "I suppose you want my honest opinion."

"Of course," I said. I started toward the stairs, but the moment I had looked forward to did not have the jubilant effect upon me that I had hoped for. Gideon had looked bored.

"I'll give it back to you after dinner," I heard him say behind me, and the door closed.

My heart was hammering so fast that I wanted to scream. I had never been so nervous before. I knew I had done the wrong thing. Gideon thought I was presuming on his friendship by making him criticize my stupid manuscript. In the few days I had known him this was the first time he had acted in such an odd and distant manner. Oh, if he only knew the real reason I had written the story and given it to him to read! If he only knew how much I loved him. At that moment I would have given anything to turn time back so that I would *not* have gone upstairs with the story.

I knew he was reading it, because he did not come down right away. When he did, it was time for dinner, and he came in and sat down at his place and kept up the usual light conversation with my mother. I sat at my place in silence, not looking at him, until I could bear the suspense no longer. Slowly I raised my eyes from my plate and unexpectedly met his gaze across the table. He winked roguishly and grinned. Covered with embarrassment, I looked back at my plate, but not before I had seen, out of the corner of my eye, that Mother had noticed the exchange between us.

As soon as he could, after dinner, Gideon whispered to me, "Meet me out on the porch."

I nodded mutely and hurried toward the kitchen with some of the dishes. Mother and Daddy were out there together, and as I started to push open the door I heard them talking, and I stopped.

"I'm glad Gideon's moving," Mother was saying. "He's been here entirely too long."

"Why, I thought you liked having him here."

"Oh, I do. I think he's perfectly charming," she said. "But it hasn't been good for Christy at all."

"What's Christy got to do with it?" Daddy said.

"Ralph, you must be blind. The child has a desperate crush on the man, and I don't think it's good for her in the least. She ought to be interested in boys her own age. Gideon is a worldly man who's old enough to be her father, but he's just immature enough to want every female he meets, no matter what her age, to be completely breathless whenever he's in the room."

"Now, I think you're pretty hard on old Gideon," Daddy protested. "All kids go through a stage where they want to be older than they are. Gideon can't help it if Christy picked on him to admire. She could pick worse people."

"He *encourages* her, Ralph."

"If he didn't like her, you'd get mad about *that*," Daddy said. "I think you're getting up a lot of steam over nothing."

"Well, I for one am glad he's leaving," Mother said firmly.

I pushed open the door with my foot and put the dishes in the sink. Mother puttered around as if nothing had happened, but before he departed, Daddy looked at me for a moment as if he had never seen me before.

After hurrying through the dishes, I went out on the porch. Gideon was sitting on the steps, but Daddy was there also. Now I would never find out what Gideon wanted to tell me, and Frank would be there any minute. I suppressed a sigh. Meanwhile, Gideon was looking through his pockets.

"I think I'm out of cigarettes," he said. "Guess I'll walk up to the drugstore and get a pack."

"Have one of mine," said Daddy.

"No thanks. I like my own brand," said Gideon. "Want to come with me, Christy? I'll buy you a soda if you haven't had too much supper."

"I can always find room for a soda," I said, and got up and followed him. Daddy lowered the paper and looked at me over his glasses. You could almost hear the wheels going round in his head.

"I thought I heard you tell your mother Frank was coming over," he said.

"Tell him to wait," I called.

It was good to get away from the house. I was beginning to feel like a goldfish.

As we walked along the street Gideon was silent, and I guessed he was trying to figure out what to say to me. He looked very thoughtful, and I glanced surreptitiously at his profile, etched against the evening sky. There was nothing the least flirtatious in his manner toward me. Why Mother thought he encouraged me was a mystery I could not fathom. He was only being nice to me, nicer than anyone else had ever been. He had even read my story, although he probably knew it would bore him.

"I put it in your room before I came downstairs," he said finally.

"Well?" I said. Now that the moment had come I felt calm.

"Have you ever been on the Orient Express?" he said slowly.

"You know I haven't."

"But you have read spy stories—Graham Greene in particular?"

"Yes," I confessed.

"Well, maybe I can forgive you the lack of originality, but the first thing every writer learns is to write about things he has at least a speaking acquaintance with. To be quite honest—and you asked me to be, remember?—and not taking into account your youth, I thought the story was appallingly bad."

"Oh," I said.

We had reached the drugstore and it was just as well to have something to do. I was completely quelled now. To tell the truth, I had secretly hoped that he would be speechless with admiration.

After we had ordered our sodas, Gideon turned and looked down at me. "Has my frankness hurt you? I'm sorry, Christy."

"It's all right," I said.

"You may improve in time," he added, "if you keep writing. And if you do keep writing after the things I've just said, then it must mean you have something in you. I honestly don't know. I'm not a good enough writer myself to judge. Maybe I'm all wrong. I could be, you know."

"No, I don't think you are."

"If you can get into your writing the thing I saw in those photographs you took—a certain individuality of style. . . . How long have you been writing, Christy?"

"Since Sunday," I said.

"Since Sunday!"

"I guess it was the inspiration of having an author in the house that made me want to turn my hand to it,"

I told him. "So you really shouldn't feel bad about telling me the truth."

Gideon laughed out loud, and the soda jerk looked at him in a quizzical way as he put our sodas on the counter.

"You are a quaint child!" he said. "I never know what you're going to do next."

Child! That did hurt—more than his truthfulness about my poor story ever could. How wrong Mother was! Gideon wasn't going to ask me to go to the dance with him. It wouldn't even occur to him to ask a child. I dipped my spoon into the soda, but if ice cream could taste like sawdust, that ice cream would have.

When we got back home, Frank was already there, and also Julie. It seemed to me that she had more work to do for Daddy than usual. Most of the time she came over to help him out only once a week or occasionally twice, but this was the third night in a row. It was perfectly obvious to me that she was chasing Gideon, but of course he had no way of knowing that this was not the usual thing.

Frank got up off the steps, with his big awkward hands at his sides, as we walked up. I felt a sense of heaviness inside me as I approached him, and already annoyance was rising up in me. Why did I have these up-and-down feelings toward him? Part of the time on

Sunday night I had enjoyed his company, and then suddenly I had wished he would go home. Yesterday when he almost kissed me in the library I had actually been thrilled for a moment. Now I disliked him again.

I tried not to watch Gideon make his way directly to the office, where the typewriter was clicking away. She's probably writing, "Now is the time for all good men to come to the aid of their country," over and over again, I thought hatefully.

"I guess you wouldn't like to go for a walk, would you?" Frank asked negatively.

I felt like saying no. Instead I made myself smile. "I like to walk," I said. Maybe he would suggest a movie. That, at least, would make the evening more endurable.

But Frank walked me right past the movie theaters as we went through the downtown section. He was probably saving all his money for college, and no doubt he was the type who'd be insulted if the girl suggested doing the paying—not that I'd ever done such a thing, but this was an emergency. Anyway, I remembered that I'd spent all my own money on the camera and the haircut.

We left the business section behind us and crossed over into the other side of town. It was nearly dark now, and from one of the houses we passed I heard a child whining that he didn't want to go to bed yet.

Frank was telling me about archaeological finds in Mesopotamia. Then he suddenly halted in his description of Sumerian civilization and said, "You're awfully quiet."

"I'm listening to you," I said, trying to sound as if I were enjoying it.

"It isn't fair for me to do all the talking. I'm sorry. But I just get carried away."

"That's all right. I guess I enjoy an intelligent conversation. Except I don't always know what you're talking about."

"You ought to read up on ancient history, Christy. It's very stimulating. I could recommend some good books to you, if you're interested."

"You do that," I said, not even bothering to hide my sarcasm. "Why don't you make a list for me?"

"That's a good idea," he said, as pleased as Punch.

He talked on while we made a circle and came back through a different section of town, winding up at the park. We walked along the edges of it, where other couples were also slowly ambling. Frank, who had had his hands in his pockets, took the nearer one out and grabbed mine.

"Ouch!" I said.

"I'm sorry," he apologized, and dropped my hand like a hot potato, putting his back in his pocket.

I stifled a giggle. "It's all right, I guess," I said, "if

you want to hold my hand, but for goodness' sake, don't squeeze it so hard."

His hand emerged again, and he took mine carefully. We walked along, swinging our arms between us.

"You must think I'm an awful flat tire," Frank said, "after Gideon Myles."

"Gideon's a lot older than you," I said cautiously.

"I hope you aren't silly like all those other girls who are in a tizzy over him. After it was in the paper about my being at your house the other night to meet him, several girls have asked me about him in the library. What's he got anyway? Even Julie. She tries not to let on, but I can tell. She's just as nuts as everyone else. And after he asked her to go to the Elks' Dance with him, she came into the house looking like a spider with a parlor full of flies."

"Gideon asked her— When? He told me he wasn't taking anybody." I tried not to act upset, but my voice came out higher than usual.

Frank stopped walking and looked down at me in the glare of a street light. "He asked her to go with him last night when he was over at our house," he said steadily, his eyes searching mine.

"Well, that's nice for her," I said lamely.

"You like him too, don't you?" he asked.

"Everybody likes him. And I'm *glad* he's taking Julie."

"No, you're not. You were hoping he'd ask you. Why, he's *old*, Christy."

"No he's not. You're just jealous."

"I wouldn't sink to jealousy," Frank said in scorn. "And to think that I thought you were different from other girls and above following the herd. If anything, you're worse. Mooning around over an *old man!*"

By that time I was seeing lights all colors of the spectrum, I was so mad. Who did he think he was to talk to me like that?

"You think you're pretty special, don't you," I retorted. "You and all your everlasting talk about archaeology. Gideon Myles is so far above you that it's positively ridiculous. He's mature and charming, but you're nothing but a *callow youth!*"

I spit out the last words as venomously as I could and walked away hurriedly. If it hadn't been unladylike, I'd have socked him. He was so smug!

Frank must have stood there for a moment, and then I heard him running after me. He grabbed my arm. "I'm disappointed in you. I certainly am."

"I don't care," I said. "And now, good night."

Frank caught up with me once more. "You're not going home alone, whatever you think of me or I think of you. I took you out for a walk, and I'm seeing you home."

"You don't have to bother," I said in icy tones.

"At least no one can say I'm not a gentleman," he informed me self-righteously.

"Ha!" I said.

We went home in silence, both of us seething. When we got to the house I went in and slammed the screen door and did not say good night again, although Frank did, and his words had a final ring. But the only effect it had on me was to make me more angry, for I felt he had had the last word.

A burst of laughter from the living room made me turn blankly in that direction. Mother, Daddy, Gideon, and Julie all looked up as they noticed me there.

"Why, Christy, what's the matter?" said Mother.

"Where's Frank?" Julie asked.

"He went home," I announced, trying to appear calm. "Good night," I added and went upstairs. Once in my room, I flung myself on the bed, weak with impotent rage. I couldn't even love Gideon at that moment; I just knew I hated Frank Fanelle.

There was a light knock at the door. "Christy," Julie's soft voice called. "Can I come in?"

"Of course," I said.

I didn't want her to. She was the last person I wanted to talk to, but then as she entered, the past did too. She was the old Julie again, the one I loved, with the old sweet smile crinkling up her eyes. But then, hadn't she always been the old Julie? It was only I who had changed.

"What happened between you and Frank?" she asked, sitting down beside me on the bed.

"We had a fight," I admitted.

"I didn't realize you were getting on that well."

"What do you mean 'getting on'? We don't get on at all. He may be your cousin, Julie, but I have to tell you he's an absolute boor!"

"We don't fight with people we're indifferent to," she said sagely.

"Well, I'm indifferent to him from now on. If you could have heard the beastly things he said—"

"I'll give him a talking to when I get home."

"No!" I almost shouted it. It would be dreadful if he told her what the argument had been about. Feeling embarrassed, I leaned back on my pillow.

"Forgive me, Christy. I forgot it was none of my business."

"It isn't that. It's just that—" Oh, what could I tell her? And if Frank told her I was jealous of her, things would never be the same again. Not that they ever could now, anyway, I thought. No matter how close a friendship you have with another girl, it can all end in an instant when you like the same man. I had learned that much.

Julie walked around the room glancing at the books

in the bookcase and looking thoughtful. "What's happened between us, Christy?"

"I don't know."

"Yes, you do," she said looking straight at me, and I couldn't return her gaze. I had to look away.

"We used to be such good friends," she said. "And now—it's Gideon, isn't it?"

Mutely, I nodded my head. It was obvious Mother had been talking to her.

"You're a victim of his charm too. I know how it is, believe me. Even though you know he does it quite deliberately, you have no defense. He's only been here —how many days?—not even a week. But what a change it's made in our lives."

"Well, anyway, he asked *you* to go to the dance," I burst out, and then I could have bitten off my tongue.

She looked at me sharply. "You mean you were hoping that he—oh, Christy!" At least she had the grace not to laugh. And her tone was so kind and pitying that it made me want to cry.

"Don't envy me too much," she said bitterly. "Whether you want to believe it or not, I'm putting myself in a position to be hurt far more than you. You're young. I'm thirty."

"What does age have to do with the way people feel? Things can hurt just as much at sixteen as at thirty, maybe worse."

"But wounds heal more quickly. And you have Frank—"

"Oh, *Frank*," I said witheringly.

"Yes, you have Frank and Barry and all the others who will come along. All the men I went to school with are married or else they've moved to greener pastures. They don't call us old maids any more, but that's what I am."

"Then you really are trying to get yourself burned," I said cruelly, "because Gideon told me he doesn't intend to get married."

"He made that clear to me, too," she said, with irony in her voice. "So you have nothing to worry about."

I sat there for a second trying to think of something to say. The trouble was I hoped she was right, while at the same time I longed to cheer her up.

"Of course, he's an awful liar," I suggested. "Maybe he's lying about getting married."

Julie laughed and the sadness went from her face. "Maybe he is," she said, and then she sat down beside me and hugged me. "Oh, Christy, how I love you. Whatever happens, please don't let's allow that big fake to come between us."

"Well, I'll try," I agreed, "but I can't promise."

"I'll accept that," she said. "Tell me, though, was that what you and Frank argued about?"

"Yes," I finally admitted. "He said Gideon was an

old man and that I was just like all the other giddy females—including you—who were swooning over him. Frank had some crazy idea that I was different from other girls, and now he's thoroughly disappointed in me."

"Frank's quite a poseur himself, if he only knew it," said Julie. "But he'll grow up too and stop being so opinionated. Maybe someday he'll be just as attractive in his way as Gideon is in his."

"Julie," I said quietly, "don't you try to matchmake like Mother does. I can't stand it."

"I don't blame you. It does make you feel rather inadequate, doesn't it? Who should know that better than I?" She patted my hand. "Go to bed now, Christy. I hope you feel better now that things have come out in the open between us. I do."

"Yes, I think I do. But it's so funny. I thought I could keep it all to myself. So far, everyone has guessed. Does everything show in my face?"

"Indeed it does," she said, smiling.

"Does *he* know?" I asked, trembling.

Julie thought for a moment. "Probably," she said. "Even if you didn't like him, he'd imagine you did, so it amounts to the same thing. He's really a very conceited man, Christy."

"How can you like him so much if you think that of him?"

"Maybe I don't like him," she said, and it was as though she had just thought of it for the first time. She went on, talking almost to herself as much as to me. "No, I don't altogether like him. But I am under his spell. And in these past days I've been studying him, because I was so fascinated. In that way, I've come to understand him a little. He's a very lonely man, Christy." She paused at the door, still looking thoughtful and slightly enigmatic, and then she opened the door and glanced back at me. "Understanding is the first step to love, I think," she said.

The room was very quiet when she left it, and I sat on the bed for a long time, thinking about what she had said. Finally I got up and undressed for bed, feeling strangely comforted.

Chapter 8

I decided to give him up. That is, if you can give up something that was never yours in the first place. But after Julie left my room that night, it seemed the most natural decision. Any chance she had of winning Gideon was so slim as to be almost nonexistent, but my own chances were even slimmer. It was ridiculous to love someone who would never love you back.

When I woke up on Thursday morning, there was an oddly dead feeling inside me, and for a minute I wondered what it was. Then I remembered my decision, but it still seemed right even if it didn't make me happy.

It was ten o'clock when I went downstairs, and of course Gideon was gone, which, I told myself, was just as well. Tomorrow he would be out of the house for good, and that would be that. Still, I dreaded tomorrow. It was going to be unbearable spending the whole day trying to ignore both Frank and Gideon.

When Margo called to ask if I wanted to go with her to pick out a new bathing suit, it suddenly occurred to me that it would help if she were to go with us. I met her in front of her house, and as we walked downtown I asked her.

"I'd love to," she said, "but Steve and I are driving out to his grandmother's for the day. If you'd only mentioned it sooner, we could both have gone. After all, I haven't met the great man yet, and you promised me I would."

"I'm sorry. I guess I've had too much on my mind lately."

"Well, I'll forgive you this time. I don't suppose I will get to meet him now, if he's moving tomorrow," she said. "To be honest, I'm a little peeved with you. What made you suddenly think of me at this late date?"

I admitted to her that I needed her as a sort of buffer because I had decided to give Gideon up. She pursed her lips, raised her eyebrows and said nothing to that.

"Besides, I'm not speaking to Frank," I added.

"Who's Frank?" she asked, her voice rising in inflection.

"Julie's cousin. You know, she brought him over to the house last Sunday night."

"Oh," said Margo.

"We had a fight last night," I said lamely.

Margo looked at me in wonderment. "You know, you amaze me, you really do. The way things have been happening to you this week, you ought to issue hourly reports," she said. "Look—it won't take me long to pick out a bathing suit, because I know just the one I want. After that, let's have a Coke, and you can bring me up to date on the life and times of Christy Collier."

We went to Lane's Department Store, and Margo tried on the bathing suit. She looked so cute in it that I was filled with an unavoidable envy. I wondered if I hadn't been wrong in taking an intellectual approach to Gideon.

"I thought you were going to buy one," she commented, as we waited for her package.

I told her about the camera, not adding that I had thought it would appeal to Gideon more, because now the whole idea seemed silly, more than silly—just plain stupid.

"Well, I admire you," she said. "I wish I had that much will power. You'll have your camera and the pictures you took long after this little rag *is* a rag. I guess I'm just the beautiful but dumb type, or at least, I'd like to be."

She giggled impishly, and I couldn't help laughing.

It was good to be with Margo. Life had seemed far too serious lately. We went to Perry's, sat down in one of the back booths, and ordered Cokes with ice cream in them.

"O.K., give," she said. "I'm dying to hear all the fascinating details on Frank and Gideon, you butterfly, you."

"Butterfly!" I groaned softly. "Far from it."

Anyway, I brought her up to date, and she listened with that typical Margo expression of wide-eyed interest combined with a sort of whimsical wisdom.

"Well, you seem to have botched everything," she said at last. "Of course, we both knew you didn't stand a chance with Gideon, but I really am sorry about Frank. For all you try to make him out as some kind of a long-winded ogre, he sounds like a perfect dear. I think I'll drop over to the library this afternoon and look him over." She looked at me boldly. "Want to come along?"

"I'm afraid I'll have to give up reading," I said sourly.

"Well, *c'est la vie,*" she said. "You know best, I suppose—or think you do. But I'm curious." And she meant what she said. We parted company at Lincoln

Street, and she turned down toward the library, leaving me to walk home alone.

"I'll call you up afterward and tell you what I think of him," she called over her shoulder.

For some reason, I longed to go with her. Not that I wanted to make up with Frank—his attitude had been unforgivable; but at the same time, I wished I could go to the library and just look right through him. However, I had enough sense to know that he would view that in another light entirely and think I really wanted to see him and was trying to make up. I wouldn't give him that satisfaction.

Listlessly, I went home and got my camera and walked over to the park and tried to get some good pictures of children at play. It made me forget for a while that I must forget about Gideon and that Frank hated me just as much as I hated him and, worst of all—the thing I had been trying not to realize—that I could not go to the Elks' Dance, because there was no one who wanted to take me.

I took several good action shots of boys playing baseball, but the one I was most proud of was of a little girl who was about two years old. She was squatting down, in that untiring way children do, pensively stroking a puppy who was with a little boy at the edge of the baseball diamond. Her face was in perfect repose, innocent and smooth, and the puppy looked so warm and fat that you could almost smell the puppy odor of him. And best of all, the lighting effect was good, subdued and filtered, with the shadows of leaves falling on the grass and on the little girl's face.

On the way home I left the roll of film to be developed, impatient at the delay, and resolving that the next thing I must do would be to learn developing myself. Thinking about it, everything else left my mind until the sound of the telephone jangled across my thoughts five minutes after I got into the house.

It was Margo. "Well, I saw him," she said.

"So?"

"You fool, you utter, utter fool!"

"Oh, Margo, honestly! I wish you wouldn't be so dramatic," I said irritably.

"He's a diamond in the rough, if I ever saw one," she said dreamily. "If I didn't like Steve so much, I sure could go for him. In fact, I could almost say that he could make me forget Steve very easily."

"You're fickle, that's what."

"*C'est la vie,*" she sighed.

"Well, you're welcome to him."

"No, I think I'll stick with Steve. I'm pretty sure of him," she said with her usual honesty. "But I do like Frank. He's very polite, and he was most helpful in finding the books I wanted."

"You know your way around that library blind-folded."

"But he didn't know that."

I digested this in silence—the beautiful-but-dumb approach. Frank would like that, I thought acidly.

Margo was still drooling. "He isn't handsome," she was saying, "but somehow it doesn't matter. I guess you'd say he's ugly in an alluring kind of way. Really, Christy, I think you ought to make up with him before some other girl gets her clutches on him. Milly Baintree was there this afternoon, and she was doing her best to distract Frank from his work. He didn't seem to mind too much, either."

"Was she there again? She certainly believes in throwing herself at him," I said.

"Well, *c'est la vie,*" was her dry comment.

Finally Margo stopped talking and I returned to my room to think about things. I was more angry than ever. Frank couldn't help it if Milly kept coming to the library, but he didn't have to enjoy it. That was the sting.

I tried to think of Gideon, so the anger would leave me, but strangely enough, the more I tried to think of Gideon, the more he escaped me and the more angry I became with Frank.

Since it was near dinnertime, I went down and helped Nora in the kitchen, for it was better to have something to do when I was in such a state. Peeling potatoes had a wonderful healing effect.

"What's got into you?" Nora asked, as she got ready to go home. "I never saw you do anything before without being asked."

"I'm reforming," I said, wishing she'd mind her own business.

"That'll be the day," she said, and put on her hat.

I could not feel annoyed at that. Nora had been insulting me since I was two years old. I managed a weak grin and watched her gather together her big worn black pocketbook. Somehow disappointment about Gideon and the dance and my petulance over Frank, combined with my picture taking that day, had made everything suddenly look novel and clear, as though I were seeing it for the first time. Nora was standing at the door, a small, dumpy woman in the dignified silk dress she wore to and from her job but carefully removed for working, in favor of a neat cotton one. Her tired face had been scrubbed clean, and her gray-streaked hair was meticulously combed up under the funny Queen Mary hat. There was something almost tangible in her complete self-respect. I wanted to preserve her that way, to touch her, as if from the touch I could gain something of that feeling. Most of all, I wanted to tell her how I felt about it, but there was no way I could put it into words that would not insult her.

"Nora," I said.

She stopped at the door and looked back.

"Could I take your picture that way?"

"Me? You want to take *my* picture?"

Pleasure and distrust fought for a moment in her face, and then she preened herself a bit as though she suddenly realized that she did look nice. "Well, all right," she said, "if it don't take too long. I have to be home, you know."

"I know," I said, running out for my camera. Luckily, I had put in a new film. I snapped in a new flash bulb on my way back. Nora was still standing at the door. When she saw me she held herself stiffly and looked serious.

"No, Nora, please don't pose. Just look natural."

She looked down at her hands. "How?" she asked.

For a second I was afraid I'd lose the mood, but I just talked to her instead. I told her to put her pocketbook back on the hook behind the door and to stand beside it and adjust her hat. "Think of all the things you have to do when you get home," I suggested.

She acted out the little scene, and when she was least expecting it, I snapped the picture. I was pretty sure I'd captured the feeling I wanted.

"Thank you," I said.

"Why, thank *you*," she told me. "You let me know how that turns out," she added. "I might want about six copies."

She smiled at me as she left, and I stood at the sink and watched through the window as she made her way down the walk, slowly, wearily—but erect like a queen.

The potatoes were soon peeled, and I was in the middle of making tapioca for dessert when I heard Gideon come in. Once my heart would have jumped into my mouth at that sound, but today it didn't. I smiled sadly to myself. Yes, it was all over. This proved it. There was a lot of talking in the hallway, and Mother, who had come downstairs, was making gleeful noises. I wondered what it was all about but made no move to join them. Anyway, the tapioca wasn't ready. Listening to the laughter and feeling lonely, I stirred the mixture patiently and saw it come to a boil. Quickly I folded it into the beaten egg whites.

Mother burst into the kitchen just as I was finishing up. "It's getting late," she was calling over her shoulder. "I've a million things to do. I wish Christy would come home." Then she saw me. "Why, you *are* home. What are you doing?"

"Getting supper."

"Oh, you darling! That'll save me a lot of time. The four of us are going out tonight."

I absorbed this information without emotion.

"Look what Gideon brought me," she said, holding out her arm. "Wasn't that sweet of him?"

Just above her wrist was a thin ebony bracelet, set in gold. It was simple and expensive-looking and quite beautiful. I sucked in a quick breath. "No wonder you were squealing," I said. "Are you going to wear it tonight?"

"Of course. What else would I do?" she said happily. "I'll take it upstairs now so I can help you. I'll be back in a minute."

He always does the right thing, I thought, as I started to make a salad. Mother's forgotten all the nasty things she said about him last night, just because of a bracelet— and because she's had her own way so far with Julie.

I was feeling pretty cynical when I heard Gideon slip into the kitchen behind me. For some reason I knew it was he, even though I didn't turn around.

"My, but you're a busy little domestic bee," he said in his slow drawl.

"Sometimes I get fits like this," I replied.

Since I didn't turn away from my work, Gideon came around and leaned against the sink and took a radish from the bunch beside the salad bowl and munched on it. He was looking down at me. I tried not to look back, but I couldn't help myself. There was a serious expression on his face, and even chewing on a radish, he managed to look sophisticated and unbearably attractive.

"I'm going to miss you, little Christy," he said.

Something churned up inside me. I tried to hold it back. My former feeling for him was still too close to the surface for comfort, but it was only because I was feeling lonely, I told myself.

"I'll still be seeing you around, I guess," I said.

"Sure," he said. "But we've had fun, haven't we?"

"Of course."

"I left a little something in your room. It isn't much, but I got your mother something, and I wanted to remember you, too, for other reasons."

"You got something for me?" I asked incredulously.

"Yes, but I don't want you to look at it now. Later. After everyone has gone out. Then you go up and look at it. All right?"

"All right," I said, trying not to show my excitement.

He took another radish, patted me on the head, and ambled out.

I thought dinner would never be over with. And then I thought they were never going to go out. But finally they did. Mother, in a new dress and sporting her new bracelet, and Daddy and Gideon went out and got into the car to pick up Julie. I heard them laughing, and then the motor started up and they drove away. I was alone in the house.

With a heart that was beating ridiculously I rushed up to my room, taking two steps at a time. There it was on the dresser—a wide, flat package, obviously a record. There was a note taped to it, and I removed it carefully and opened it.

In his handwriting, scrawling and masculine, it said: "For Christy, in memory of a bright, shining day. I will always think of you when I hear 'Greensleeves,' and I hope it will remind you of your admirer, Gideon."

My fingers trembled as I turned on my phonograph and took the record out of its envelope. Carefully I placed it on the spinning turntable and lowered the needle. Piercingly sweet, the song filled my small room, Old English was the strain, and the memory was of a bright, shining day. Sitting there on the floor beside it, I leaned my head against the side of the bed and listened achingly.

Oh, Gideon, I thought, you always *do* do the right thing, don't you?

Chapter 9

It was the Fourth of July, and when I awoke the sun had not yet risen. The morning was still misty, but a wind was blowing the mist away as the birds twittered sleepily in the trees. It looked as if it would be a nice day. When I heard Mother stirring I got dressed and went downstairs to help her. There was no lunch to pack, because Gideon had told us he had prepared for us, so there was nothing to do but get breakfast ready and gather up our bathing suits. Before Julie, her father, and Frank arrived with the truck and the furniture, I snatched a moment alone with Gideon to thank him for the record.

"I thought you'd like it," he said.

"I'll cherish it," I told him brightly—too brightly, I thought. It would never do to let him know how much I really meant what I said.

He was sitting on the porch steps beside me when the truck drove up, and I was glad of that. I did not want to be by myself when Frank and I met again, and to have Gideon beside me would show him how little I cared for his opinions.

Julie hopped out of the truck. She had on Bermuda shorts, a neat plaid shirt, and a dark red scarf tied around her head. She looked jaunty and cute, much more so than I did in my slacks. I had thought of wearing shorts, but since I intended to tramp around the woods with my camera, I had wanted to protect my legs. Now I regretted my decision, but of course it was too late.

"Are you ready?" she asked gaily.

"Don't we look it? We've been waiting for you since dawn," said Gideon, who had been up only half an hour.

I listened to their byplay and tried to look pleasant, but I was conscious that Frank had made no move to get out of the truck. He was sulking.

"Do you want to ride in the truck with Frank and me?" asked Mr. Fanelle, who had meanwhile been eyeing my haircut in silent wonder.

I like Mr. Fanelle, and I hated to refuse him anything, but I was bound and determined that I would not ride in that truck with Frank. I was looking at him help-lessly, when Julie came to my rescue.

"She's going to ride in the car, in the back seat with Edna and me," she said. "There's no need for her to be uncomfortable."

"It's not that long a ride," said Mr. Fanelle. "I thought Christy and I could have one of our old con-fabs. I haven't seen you in a month of Sundays, girl."

Freed of the necessity of refusing his offer, I grinned at him. "We can talk when we get out there," I said.

Before we left, Julie took me to one side. "Don't worry about Frank," she whispered. "He's not going to sulk all day. As a matter of fact, I know he's dying to make it up, but he's stubborn."

"I don't care if he is."

"Don't *you* sulk," she said.

All the way to the lake they talked about the Elks' Dance, until I was sure I had it coming out of my ears.

And once Gideon turned around and looked at me. "I guess you know," he told me, "that Miss Fanelle, looking so self-satisfied over there in the corner, has roped me into going."

"You aren't as strong as you thought you were, are you?" I managed to say teasingly.

"What man ever is?" said Daddy fervently. "Women!"

Gideon laughed, and winked at me. "Have you

broken down Frank's resistance yet? He told me lugu-
briously that he considered dances a middle-class Bac-
chanalia, and that he would never waste his time at one.
But I'll bet that one come-hither glance from Christy's
eyes will have him conforming in no time. Am I right,
Christy?"

"No. Frank probably can't even dance," I said scorn-
fully.

"Yes, he can," Julie told me quietly. "And he's also
been practicing with me on the sly."

I could not look at her. Was it Milly Baintree? Had
he asked her? Or did he plan to? Suddenly I realized
that Frank was my only chance to go to the dance. If
that failed, I would never dance with Gideon, and the
summer would end, and I would be left with nothing
but ashes.

Gideon's cottage was set in a little glade looking out
over a small beach, with a tiny boathouse at one side.
It was an old house, sturdily built of weathered stone,
with a green roof. We crossed over a terrace into a
bright living-dining room. On one side of it was a
compact electric kitchen, with a wood stove for times
when the power was off, and on the other side was the
bedroom, with a small bath. To me, it was a perfect
dream house, and for just a moment I allowed myself to
picture a snowy winter evening with the wind howling

outdoors, and Gideon and me sitting snugly by the fireplace. But it was only for a moment. Frank brought in an easy chair and placed it in front of the fireplace.

Julie sat down in it. "Oh, this is lovely," she said.

The picture was shattered.

As I had suspected, Gideon had cleaned and painted already, so there wasn't much to do except bring in the furniture. Mother and Julia made a fuss over the things I had picked out.

"They're in very good taste, darling," Mother said. "Sometimes you really show signs of maturity."

I frowned at her patronizing tone, and then I caught Gideon smiling impishly at me from the doorway, as if to say that he knew, if they didn't, that I was no longer a child.

When everything was in place, Gideon started to set a fire in the outside fireplace. It was too early to eat, but he was full of the pride of ownership and seemed to want to be doing something. As Julie was helping him, I walked away toward the beach, where Frank was standing alone at the water's edge. Not wanting to whitewash myself, I have to admit that my motive in doing so was very ulterior.

He did not make it easy for me. Although he knew I was standing there, he deliberately turned his back a little more, picked up a pebble, and sent it skipping across the water.

"Very good," I said.

He put his hands in his pockets.

"Both of us can't be pigheaded," I said. "One of us has to give in, and I guess it has to be me. After all, it isn't fair to the others for us to be glaring at each other all day."

"I wasn't glaring," said Frank, and he did not sound angry. He turned around and looked at me, the reflected light of the sun flashing in his glasses. I blinked. "Excuse me," he said. "I don't really need them now." He took them off, and his eyes had that naked look that people always get when they habitually wear glasses and then take them off. For a moment they met my own eyes, and I saw that there was no anger there, just an odd moroseness and a deep mystery that made him seem strangely attractive.

I held out my hand. "I'm willing to be friends," I said. "Are you?"

He did not answer but just kept on looking at me in that sad way. I felt myself flushing. If only he'd say something. "Well, we can pretend anyway," I said, "just for today."

"I never pretend," said Frank, "about anything."

"Well, all right, then." I lowered my hand.

"I mean," he explained, "if we're friends again, that's good. But if we have to pretend, it's no go."

"*I* want us to be friends," I said patiently.

"So do I. But maybe after you know everything you won't want to be."

"Now what does *that* mean?"

He started to speak, and then he glanced toward the house. Mother and Daddy were running down toward us in their bathing suits.

"I'll race you out to the float," said Daddy. "Eyow! That water's cold!"

"And the wind isn't going to make you feel any warmer once you're wet," Mother shouted.

"Let's go somewhere where we can talk," said Frank.

He started up toward the house, past Julie and Gideon and into the woods beyond. I followed him curiously as he made his way along a little meandering path that led nowhere. But it was green and cool after the bright sunlight on the lake, and the bird sounds were muted and soothing. Finally we came to a small clearing where soft grass made a natural carpet. He sat down and motioned for me to follow suit. I lay down on my stomach and listened to the stillness. Then, suddenly, a great burst of wind fell upon the trees above us, and for a few seconds the air was alive with the roar, like a huge wave breaking against a shore. The trees bent with it, bowed in reverence before it. I had never heard the sea, but I knew it must be like that. And then it was gone, leaving a silence more profound than before, although the leaves still shuddered in remembrance.

"How wonderful," I whispered.

Frank looked down at me, and his face broke into one of those rare smiles, which transformed him.

"Yes," he said.

We shared the moment for a little while, looking at each other without speaking again, as though words would break the spell, until finally I had to look away. I did not know why, but I felt a perverse compulsion to cut the tiny thread of closeness that seemed to entwine us—as if it were something I could not cope with.

"Listen," said Frank.

It was coming again like a train off in the distance, tearing onward relentlessly. Trembling a little, I looked down. In front of me the tiniest spider's web I had ever seen hung suspended between two grasses, and in the middle of it was a minute brown spider. The roaring wind came on; above us the trees arched in submission, and there before me the little web billowed in the gale. But with all the buffeting, it did not break, and the small brown spider clung to it, secure.

When the wind had passed, I picked up my camera, which lay on the ground beside me. "I hope I can get it," I said.

Frank knelt down beside me and looked at the perfect little thing, and he was silent as I took two pictures of it.

"Say a prayer," I said. "If it's good, it'll be the best one yet."

"I didn't know you were a camera bug," he said at last, when I was finished, but there was respect in his voice.

"There are lots of things you don't know about me," I said. "Not everything I do is stupid."

"Don't rub it in," he said quickly.

"All right, I won't. But what was it you wanted to tell me that was supposed to be so upsetting that I'd hate you for it?" I smiled when I said it. In all the loveliness of the things we had just shared, I did not think I could ever hate him again.

The strange look came back into his face, and he sat there glaring at me in his usual way. "I asked Milly Baintree to go to the Elks' Dance with me," he said.

I must have gasped, for when he said that, something died inside me. Although I despised myself for it afterwards, I turned my face away.

"What are you telling me that for?" I asked, muffling my voice in the grass. "I guess it's your privilege to ask whomever you want."

"But I don't want to take her. She's a silly, idiotic girl. It was you I wanted to take, all along."

"For someone who doesn't like dances, you sure get around," I said, gathering myself together a little.

"As soon as I heard about the dance I made up my mind to ask you. I was going to ask you that night we argued, but then you were so high and mighty that the next day I asked Milly. I don't know why I did. I wanted to punish you, I guess. All I succeeded in doing, though, was to punish myself. For Pete's sake, what am I going to do?"

"I guess you'll take Milly to the dance and be nice to her. It isn't her fault, you know."

I felt very magnanimous saying that, even if it wasn't true. I hoped Milly would have a perfectly miserable time.

"You don't really care, do you?" he said.

"Of course I do," I replied, in a sickeningly cheerful tone. "It would have been fun going to a dance with a misan—misan—"

"Misanthrope," Frank said dryly. "Is that what you think of me?"

"You just try to be one," I told him kindly. "You're really very good. And it would have been fun, Frank. Thank you for at least wanting to take me." My voice almost broke at that. What comfort was there in knowing someone had wanted to take me? Would that help when everyone went to the dance but me, the dance where I might have danced with Gideon? And not only that, Gideon would know what a failure I was.

I couldn't keep up the pretense any longer. I got up and brushed the grass off my slacks.

"Let's go back," I said. "I'm dying for a swim, aren't you?"

Chapter 10

As far as I was concerned, the rest of the day was a dud. When I think back on it, I wonder why I never had any ambition to be an actress, for the act I put on was worthy of an Academy Award. I laughed, I splashed water on Gideon and Frank, I raced everyone to the float and won. When it was time to eat, I forced down the food as though I really wanted it, and I took candid snapshots of everyone. Later, when the moon came up and we all sat around a campfire on the beach, it was my voice that was loudest in song.

I thought that day would never end. What a wonderful relief it was to get home to my own room and my quiet bed, where the tiredness and the desperation could sweep over me in solitude.

It was awfully hard to face the fact that I, Christy Collier, who had always had a date for everything, did not have anyone to take me to the Elks' Dance. Now I knew how it felt to be a wallflower—less than a wall-flower—but those girls, at least, did not have the added humiliation of being has-beens. I had always felt secure in having a reasonable amount of popularity; I never would again. It would have been nice if I had been able to hate Frank as I had once, but in a way, I realized he had paid me an odd type of compliment when he made a date with another girl to make me jealous. No, I did not hate him any longer. It was Milly Baintree I disliked instead, even if she was just an innocent bystander in the whole affair.

At last sleep came to me, a deep sleep as though I had been drugged. I guess people sleep that way when there is no hope left—it is a kind of escape.

In the morning I awoke to silence, for Mother and Daddy were still asleep, and Gideon was not there to fill the house with life. He was twenty miles away; he might as well have been in China. And it was raining, which was just as it should be.

I went downstairs, fixed some orange juice, and drank two glassfuls; that was all the breakfast I could swallow. I went outside. It was raining steadily, the kind of a rain that keeps up all day. In the grayness, the green of the grass and the leaves stood out with special vividness, and even the tree trunks looked browner with the water dripping down them. Suddenly I became aware that lately I had been more conscious of beauty. I was noticing things around me that had been there all the time, but to which I had always been blind. Perhaps it was the renewed interest in photography that had done this for me, but I was more inclined to think that it was Gideon's influence and my love for him. Had it only been a week ago today when I met him? It seemed much longer.

When I reached Margo's house, she was washing the breakfast dishes. I dried them for her, and she told me about her day with Steve. She asked about what had happened to me, but I gave her a warning look, as her mother was nearby, and I didn't want her to hear.

"Mum's the word," Margo whispered.

As soon as we could we went up to her room. Margo shut the door and plopped down on the bed. "Well, give," she said. "Did you make up with Frank?"

Margo has a window seat in her room which I have always loved. I curled up on it, half sheltered by the ruffled curtains, and looked out at the rainy back yard. A little gust of wind blew through the apple tree, turning over the leaves. The undersides of them were a silvery green in the rain. The sight of them made me feel very sad.

"Yes, I made up with him," I said.

"Well, that's good," she commented. "I hope you've sense enough to be glad."

"I suppose so."

"You're a queer duck," Margo said. "Did he ask you to go to the dance? The odds are right for it, don't you think?"

"The odds *were* right for it, but I muffed it. To get even with me after our fight, he went and asked Milly Baintree."

"Oh, no! Oh, Chris, what are you going to do?"

I looked over at her miserably. With Margo I did not have to hide my real feelings. "I guess I don't go."

"That's impossible. You *have* to go. There must be someone left in town who'd take you."

But I had gone over in my mind already the names of all the boys I had dated during the past year. Two of them were out of town, one had moved away, another was going steady now, and Barry Preston hadn't called me up since last Saturday, when I had failed to be impressed by his condescension in noticing me.

"Barry!" Margo exclaimed as if she had read my thoughts.

"Fat chance!"

"Well, it's true you weren't exactly flattering last week when we all went out, but he may have forgotten it by now. I don't *think* he's asked anybody else to go to the dance, because Steve mentioned our making it a double date, and he *didn't* say who the other girl would be." Margo looked at me in excitement as she sat up on the bed with her neck out like a bird's. "Chris, I'm *sure* I can manage it. Oh, let me try, will you? Steve's working today down at the Truex Market. I'll go and see him this afternoon and arrange something. Just leave it to little old Miss Fix-it."

She looked so pleased with herself that I forced myself to smile, although I didn't feel like it. It was embarrassing to have your friend arrange a date for you. It made me feel as small as an insect. Yet I knew it had to be that way, even though it meant facing the horrid fact that she might fail.

"I'll go right now," Margo announced, getting off the bed.

"You're a pal," I said.

"I know it," she replied, and then in the middle of putting on her lipstick, she turned around and gave me a shrewd look. "You really don't deserve it. I hope all this has taught you a lesson—be nice to everybody, especially men. Even the conceited Barry Prestons of this world can come in handy." Then she laughed. "Listen to me. You've got me doing it. A week ago we both thought Barry was Apollo himself. What's happened?"

"Three things happened; their names are Gideon, Frank, and Steve." I laughed myself, and it felt good, for the tension lifted.

"Yes, Steve," said Margo softly. "He's such a darling. If it weren't for him, I'd be right over in the library this minute. Honey, you'd better stake a claim on Frank, because I have a feeling that when word of him gets around you're going to have a lot more than just Milly Baintree to contend with."

"You know, I think you're right," I admitted, thinking of Frank's brown eyes and their penetrating angry glance, which had so often been directed at me yesterday.

"As for Gideon Myles," Margo continued, chasing the thought of Frank right out of my head, "I think it's a good thing he moved away. He hasn't been good for you at all."

It was better not to contradict her. Too much depended on her good opinion of me right now. I tried to look cheerful as I waved good-by to her in front of her house. She walked down the street toward the market, and I turned my head toward home, walking slowly through the misty rain. I decided not to let myself hope too much that Margo and Steve could convince Barry that he should take me to the dance. That would be too good to be true, I felt in my depressed, wallflower state of mind, and, as Margo had said, much more than I deserved. Resigned to my condition, I looked ahead hopelessly at the dreary, endless days to come.

Margo called later in the day to tell me that Steve had promised to work on Barry, and with this I had to be content. Then Frank called and asked me to go to the movies with him that night, and I agreed with haste. Maybe I would have to miss the dance, but at any rate, this was no reason to sit home alone on Saturday night.

After the movies we stopped at Perry's. Frank sat across from me in the booth, and I saw him take some change out of his pocket and count it out of the corner of his eye as he held it against his hip. Poor Frank, I thought. Taking a girl out to a movie must cut deeply into the little bit of money he allowed himself out of his earnings for pleasure. Perhaps he had given up something he wanted or even lunch, to pay for this outing tonight. I wished idly that it wouldn't be slightly improper for a girl to offer to go Dutch, but the thought ended there. Just looking at the proud, stubborn set of his shoulders told me what his answer to that would be.

"I liked the picture, didn't you?" I said. "It was nice of you to invite me."

"It was O.K.," he replied, "if you like mass entertainment."

"I guess I'm just ignorant enough to enjoy it." I sighed to myself. Frank was such a snob at times.

"Besides," he added, "what else is there to do in a small town?"

"There are lots of things, and most of them don't

cost anything. In the summer there's swimming, and in the winter there's ice skating and, of course, school sports—which are often free. For goodness' sake, Frank," I said, "I know you're saving your money for school, and honestly, I don't want you to feel you have to take me out on expensive dates—especially when you have such a low opinion of American movies."

"I didn't mean that exactly," he said penitently. "I liked seeing it with you. Anyway, we can't go swimming at night very well."

"We could stay home and see a free *old* movie on television—or go for a walk."

"You mean you'd be happy just going for a walk with me?"

"Why not?"

Frank looked steadily at me across the table, with that stiff, angry stare of his that was becoming very familiar to me. "Do you know what you're saying?" he asked in an odd voice. I shook my head. "You're as much as saying that you're my girl."

I gasped and did not know how to answer him for a minute, and then I shook my head again slowly. "No, no, I didn't mean that at all. Why, Frank, we only met each other last Sunday."

"A lot can happen in a week," he said solemnly.

How well I knew that—but I said, "Anyway, I promised Daddy I wouldn't go steady with anyone until after high school, at least."

"He's right," Frank said, and nodded in a judicious manner. "Just the same, you are, and I'll think of you that way."

He raised his head and looked about him with a victorious look on his face. Once, that proud almost arrogant gesture would have irritated me, or at the least, amused me. Now my heart just went out to him in a pitying way. What a vulnerable boy he was!

Then as my glance followed his gaze, I grew cold all over. Barry Preston had just walked into the store. He was with another boy, and they were talking and not noticing anyone. They sat at the counter, and from the bits of conversation that drifted over, I gathered that they had been to the night baseball game in the city. I sipped my Coke with one eye on him, hoping he would notice me with Frank. He didn't have to know that Frank already had a date for the dance. Maybe it would be just the push he needed to make him hurry up and ask me.

Frank lit up his pipe and settled back to enjoy it while I tried to make my Coke last as long as possible. Barry turned around on the stool to leave, and my mind all the time was willing him to look my way.

He did! Seeing Frank, he hesitated, but then he walked over to us. "Hi, Christy," he said.

"Hi." I flashed my most winning smile at him.

"Say, you look cute with your hair cut. I heard about it."

"Thanks," I said, really striving with the smile. I have one, rather weak, dimple and I hoped it was in evidence.

"By the way, I was talking to Steve this afternoon and I . . ." He looked over at Frank. "Well, I'll call you tomorrow. Right after church?"

"Sure thing," I said, with just the right touch of casualness.

I introduced him to Frank, who nodded coldly. Barry gave me a farewell grin, and departed, and Frank bit down hard on his pipe and glowered. His balloon of triumph had burst.

"I guess I *was* presumptuous," he muttered.

"Well, a little," I admitted. "Besides, Frank, I want to go to that dance, and if I'm your girl, why are you taking Milly Baintree?"

"Oh, all right. You've made your point. I guess I had it coming."

"Anyway," I said, "I've known Barry for ages. Do you expect me to start ignoring all my old friends?"

"I guess I'd like that fine," he said, but he managed to grin.

Remembering Gideon's advice about playing the field,

I decided to get one thing straight right away, or Frank was going to turn out to be a handful.

"If we're going to see each other again, you're going to have to remember one thing," I said firmly. "You're not to give other boys that 'hands off' look you just gave Barry. I want to go out with other boys. If I don't, I won't have any fun in my last year of high school, and you'll probably be too busy studying then to see much of me."

"You're right about that," he said with dignity. "I don't want to be selfish about it."

He took my hand as we left Perry's and headed toward home. It was still raining lightly, but we had brought no umbrella, as both of us had agreed before we left home that we scorned umbrellas.

"I love rain," I said.

"I knew you'd be the kind of girl who did.'

We walked home very slowly, and for once he did not bring up the subject of archaeology. I almost wished he would, because I was afraid I had scared him off it when we had our argument.

"When I made fun of archaeology that night," I said, "I didn't really mean it. I'm sorry."

"You were just mad. I understand," he said tolerantly. And then he suddenly asked, "But the part about Gideon—I'm still a little concerned about that. Are you over it now, Christy?"

He had stopped beneath a tree just below Margo's house. It was dark and I couldn't see his face, but I could hear his breath and the sound of the rain dripping off the leaves.

"I—I don't know," I said softly.

I heard him give a slow, quiet sigh. Then he said, "You probably can't help it. I wish he'd go away, though."

"Sometimes I almost wish he would too," I said. "Far, far away."

"If you wish that, then you're not over it." He did not sound angry, just unhappy. We were still standing beneath the tree, but Frank made no move to go on. Suddenly I felt the back of his hand pressing lightly against my cheek. "Your face is cool and wet with rain," he said, and I felt a shock at the tenderness in his touch and in his voice. I was sure he was going to kiss me. If he had, it might have made a difference. Maybe the things that happened later would never have happened at all. But he didn't. Instead, he took my hand and walked me firmly home. At the door he patted the hand and let it go.

"I nearly kissed you back there," he said gruffly, and I could see that the old Frank was back, not the tender Frank of the darkness under the trees, but the opinionated one with the unwavering convictions.

"For a minute," he went on, "I thought I could kiss

the image of him out of your mind. But then, I would always be wondering whether I had succeeded or not. Much as I want to, Christy, I'm never going to kiss you as long as you're still mooning over Gideon Myles."

I stifled a retort with great effort. The conceited thing! Withholding his kiss, as if it were something sacred, because my mind wasn't in what he considered the proper condition. It was lucky I hadn't brought the umbrella, for I would have hit him with it. He probably thought I *wanted* him to kiss me!

But later, in my room, common sense overwhelmed me, and I lay on my bed and howled with laughter, until Mother came in to see what was the matter. I really wished I could tell her, for it was too rich a joke to keep to myself. But I just said, "Oh, Frank gets the craziest ideas. You know how he is."

Mother smiled vaguely. "He is an odd boy, isn't he?"

At that I laughed all the more, and she finally went back to bed, shaking her head at the mystery.

But the thing that made it even more ridiculous to me was that I *had* wanted him to kiss me.

Chapter 11

After church Sunday I hung around the telephone in a cold sweat waiting for Barry's call. Mother kept urging me to go upstairs and change my clothes, and I kept putting her off. When the phone finally did ring it jolted me nearly out of my skin. I stood there and let it jangle three times until Mother came in and said, "For heaven's sake, Christy, answer the phone. Are you out of your mind?" She walked away in agitation as I slowly picked up the receiver.

It was Barry. He asked me to go swimming with him and Steve and Margo that afternoon, to which I agreed, after the proper amount of hesitation, but I thought he would never get to the point. However, at last, he said, "Say, you aren't dated up for the Elks' Labor Day Dance, are you? I thought it might be fun if we could make it a foursome with Margo and Steve. But maybe you've already agreed to go with that fellow I saw you with in Perry's last night."

"I haven't said I'd go with him," I said, which certainly wasn't a lie.

"Well, does that mean you'll go with me then?"

I let out a long, slow breath. "I guess it does," I said. "In fact, I'd love to go with you, Barry."

And so it was settled. I had really suffered for that invitation, and right then and there, I vowed I would never let myself get in such a predicament again.

Nevertheless, in the nearly two months that followed I found myself in a stranger dilemma. Since I had promised to go to the dance with Barry, I felt that I owed it to him to double-date with Margo and Steve. Not that Barry had a crush on me—he had too big a crush on himself ever to arrive at that state—but I had learned that his pride was easily hurt. There were too many girls in town who looked at Barry with worship in their eyes for him to put up with anyone who acted indifferent, and this was how I learned that nine tenths of the secret of popularity consisted in being a subtle flatterer. When I confided this discovery to Julie, she told me I was too young to be so cynical, but then she laughed and added, "I wish I had learned it at your age, though."

In between going out with Barry, I managed to juggle in some dates with Frank. They were different from my dates with Barry—discussions, really, more than anything else. Frank was still a little jealous of my going out with someone else, but when he began to realize that Barry and I were just good friends, he seemed to feel better about it. However, never again after that night in the rain did Frank make any attempt to be romantic or try to kiss me, which was all right with me. When he was being his usual self—opinionated and pedantic—I didn't feel like kissing him anyway.

Besides, Frank also knew I saw Gideon occasionally. Gideon often came to dinner, sometimes with Julie and sometimes without her. Several times I went with my parents out to his cottage. I saw him just enough to keep him constantly in my mind. After I ran into him accidentally on the street one day, I ever afterward kept imagining that I saw him ahead of me or in a crowd, and my knees would get weak until I realized it wasn't he.

But this heady experience of always looking for Gideon in crowds while at the same time there were two boys to take me out was not always fun. Once I even complained to Margo that it was very nerve-racking trying to keep Frank and Barry from being jealous of each other, and still seeing Gideon at every available opportunity. By this time, of course, Margo had figured out that I still cared for him.

"You have to pay a price for popularity," she said. "But *c'est la vie!* You'd be more wretched not having any dates. Or have you forgotten?"

No, I hadn't forgotten. Sometimes I got goose flesh just remembering what it was like to feel that no one cared about me. When school started, I told Margo, I was going to be nicer to girls who had no dates and maybe help them get some of their own.

"Don't be so sickeningly smug," she told me tartly.

She was right, of course. I was smug. But there were often times, too, when I felt very unsure of myself. As the summer days sped past, I knew that Gideon's days in Peabody were drawing to a close. And I was no nearer than before to my dream of making him love me. If I could somehow imprint my face on his memory so that it would haunt him wherever he went, then I could be sure that he would come back someday and ask me to marry him.

For a while I had a favorite daydream in which he turned to me and said tremulously, "Oh, Christy, I can't fight it any longer. I know there's a great difference in our ages, but I can't get you out of my thoughts. If I promise to wait for you and to come back for you next spring after graduation, will you marry me then?" But although I planned the words for him carefully, I couldn't quite imagine his voice saying them, and then, in superstitious horror, I stopped pretending—however comforting it was—because I was afraid that by dreaming it so vividly I might prevent it from coming true.

My only comfort was that Julie seemed to be getting nowhere with him either. Their relationship was gay and light. He always treated her like a pal, the same way he treated me, and I saw little there to be envious of. Julie confirmed my suspicions by the strained look that came over her face at times when Gideon wasn't there or wasn't looking. It made me pity her so much that I was sometimes in the paradoxical position of almost wishing that the thing I dreaded most would actually happen.

Meanwhile, the summer days waned, and the August nights hinted at fall frosts to come. School would start again the Tuesday after Labor Day, and, Gideon told us, he was going to leave for New York that same day.

Labor Day dawned at last, a bright crisp day with a blue, cloudless sky, and I spent most of it getting ready for the dance that night. My hair had grown out a bit since I had it cut, and as long as it remained soft and fluffy I let it stay that way. After dreadful fears that Mother would make me wear my childish pink junior prom dress, she had come around finally and let me have a new one. And how I loved that dress! Although not long, it was chiffon, made in a very simple Grecian style and had no sleeves. It was sort of green, with hints of blue in it—sea green. And it was Gideon who saw me in it before anyone else.

He dropped in on his way to pick up Julie, and I came down the stairs to tell him Mother and Daddy were still dressing. He let me make my entrance in silence, with a smile on his face and a light in his eyes that I was sure had never been there for me before. When I reached him at the bottom of the stairs he took my hand and, holding it up, twirled me around.

Then he stood back and looked at me again, with his chin in his hand. "What is it you remind me of?" he said musingly. "There's a quality about you tonight, but at the moment its exact description escapes me. If I think of what it is, I'll tell you when we have our dance. You will save me one dance, won't you, Christy?"

I swallowed helplessly. "Yes," I said demurely.

Soon afterward he was gone, but at least I had that to look forward to.

The dance was held in the hotel ballroom, which has a garden in back of it, and the French doors were opened at that end so that the cool, fall-like air could drift in over the dancers. The Elks had also taken over the dining room, so the doors were opened between the rooms. When I arrived with Barry, Margo, and Steve, the caterers were already getting things ready, and the band was tuning up. It was exciting, more exciting than a school dance ever could be. Held for charity, it was just about the most important event that took place in Peabody all year, and I was attending it at last! Of all the dances I ever go to in my life, that one will be the one I remember the longest. It will stand out in my memory like a sweet perfume that never fades away.

By the time Margo and I had checked our wraps and made sure we looked all right, the first dance of the evening had begun, and Barry, looking very handsome in white, came to claim me. There were still a lot of people who hadn't arrived, and we were one of the first couples to start dancing. It was nice having that big shiny floor almost to ourselves, and we danced well together. Both of us knew it. Out of the corner of my eye I watched for Gideon.

But it was Frank that I saw. He looked extremely uncomfortable in a stiff new suit, and he scowled when I smiled over at him. Then Milly came in, and he said something to her. She nodded her head and after that they danced, too. Frank seemed to be counting to himself, but gradually he relaxed, and I was glad of that. I really did want him to have a good time.

However, when he danced with me later he stiffened up again and stepped on my toe. "I'm sorry," he muttered.

"Why don't you relax? You were doing all right with Milly."

"Milly doesn't matter."

"Well, if I do matter, then please relax," I said. "You act like you're scared of me or something."

"I am. Scared stiff." He managed a weak smile. "You look so pretty tonight, so—so unattainable," he said.

"I'm still the same girl I was yesterday. Hold me tighter," I said. "That's fine."

We were doing better when I happened to look up and see Gideon dancing with Julie nearby. He gave me a wink, and then it was I, not Frank, who missed a step. Frank glanced around and saw him, and when he looked back into my eyes, I could feel a guilty flush stealing over my face. Propelling me doggedly around the floor, Frank did not say anything else until the music ended, and then he said, "Do you have the next dance with Barry?"

"Yes. Why?"

"You ought to be glad of that. You make a better impression dancing with him."

I still felt the sting of his words as Barry came for me and led me out on the floor again in his graceful way, but the feeling did not remain long. I put it out of my mind forcefully. I was not going to let Frank spoil this night for me.

Then as he danced past us with Mother, Gideon

whispered to me, "The next one, Christy?" and I nodded in reply. I thought my heart would burst. And when my dance with Barry ended and I saw Gideon striding toward me in his brown slacks and white coat, I knew no other male in the place could hold a candle to him. He was the handsomest man there.

"I know now," he said, taking my hand, "what it is you remind me of. Remember the story by Hans Christian Andersen? You look like the little mermaid who gave up immortality for love."

He said it lightly, but he did not know how true it could be. I knew then I could give up anything for him, even if it meant having every step I took feel as if knives were sticking into the soles of my feet.

He took me in his arms, and it was just as I had imagined it would be. He danced like a god. His arms were firm, and I felt like a feather floating in the air. We just danced and didn't say anything, and that is the best way. Once, though, he gently reached up and brushed back a lock of my short hair which had come out of place. I know that was a very little thing, but I kept remembering it afterward. Gideon is an extremely masculine man, but at the same time there is something very tender about him, and that was what made me love him most. A strong man who can be gentle is the most wonderful kind there is.

"Christy, that was very nice," he said sincerely, when

the dance was over, and I just stood looking up at him hating to tear my eyes away. Strangely enough, he seemed to have the same reluctance.

But then Steve broke the spell by tapping me on the shoulder.

"We have the next dance," he said.

I gave Gideon one last smile and turned to Steve and we walked away. My heart was thumping like a thousand pinball machines. It was awfully hard to walk away. Gideon was like a magnet, and I was a little steel shaving.

He had not asked me to dance again, but during intermission, when I was sitting in the dining room with the crowd of kids, I saw him excuse himself from the people he was with and come over to me.

"How about another dance later, Christy?"

"Of course," I said, and he went back to his own table. Some perversity made me glance at Frank, although I did not want to. He was staring moodily down at his plate.

However, when Gideon came to claim his dance, he seemed preoccupied. "Let's sit this one out," he said. "Have you been out in the garden yet?"

"No." Puzzled, I went with him. Behind me I could feel Frank's eyes boring into my back. Maybe he wasn't even looking—maybe I was just imagining it—but that was the way it seemed to me. Why I should have thought of Frank at that moment, anyway, I didn't know. Besides, there was nothing *wrong* in sitting out a dance with Gideon in the garden.

I was glad no one was out there. It was quiet under the willow trees, with just the sound of the band in the background playing a popular waltz, and the trickling of a little fountain. Around the fountain was a bed of zinnias, and you could dimly see their colors in the faint light from the ballroom that filtered through the low-hanging pale leaves.

We sat down on a white iron bench that faced the fountain. Gideon was still deep in thought.

"A penny for your thoughts," I said, wondering why he had brought me out here if he just wanted to think.

Gideon turned to me. "I was just thinking of—nothing," he said, and he sat there some more, but he was looking at me now, apparently studying me.

It seemed impossible that he could not hear my heart. I was almost certain that he was getting ready to ask me to marry him, and I lowered my eyes in confusion.

"What a funny little thing you are," he said at last. "Does it amuse you to have all the boys falling over themselves the way you've made them do tonight?"

In spite of myself, I felt the corners of my mouth turning up. "I'd be a liar if I said I didn't like it."

"If I were younger I'd give them a run for their money," he said firmly, and then he grinned—the old urbane grin. "Or if you were older," he added slyly.

I managed not to squirm uncomfortably, but I felt restless suddenly. Things were not going the way I wanted them to. He was teasing me. Had he come out here with me just to do that? If I live a hundred years, I thought, I'll never be able to understand why he does the things he does.

Determined to turn the conversation another way, I said, "I'm going to hate to see you go, Gideon." And suddenly I realized the thing I had been avoiding all evening. This would be the last time I would see him or hear his gently bantering voice—at least, the last time until next summer, and that seemed so far away as to be almost never. "You—you will come back next year?" I asked, and heard my voice quaver as I said it.

"You can count on that," he said. He stood up and held out his hand to me. "Dance?" he asked.

I arose and walked into his arms. It seemed so natural. We danced a few steps in front of the fountain, and then Gideon stopped and looked down at me, still with his arm around me. Afraid to speak for fear of spoiling the mood, I gazed up at him. I shall never forget the look in his eyes as they met mine. They seemed to look deep into me, and there was nothing mocking or teasing about them, just a kind of sadness that I could not understand.

"*Auf Wiedersehen*, Christy," he said.

I started to say something, but it never came out, for suddenly he bent his head and kissed me on the lips. It was a light kiss, almost a benediction, but for just a second I felt his arms tighten around me. Then he let me go and held me away from him and continued to look at me with that strange piercing look. Dazed and almost hypnotized, I returned his gaze, and it seemed to me that I heard a whirring of wings, but it was only a breeze stirring the willow trees.

"The music has stopped, Christy," he said softly. "Someone will be looking for you."

Yes, the music had stopped. Perhaps the world had stopped turning. But I came back to earth a bit when I heard Barry's voice calling me from the doorway. "Hey, Christy, it's our dance."

I turned away and went to him, still not having said anything to Gideon, and the light in the ballroom blinded me for a minute. Barry did not seem to notice anything, however, for he was saying, "We're all going to leave after this dance. Steve and Margo want to be at the drive-in before it gets too late, and your mother told me to tell you she wants you home and in bed by twelve. School tomorrow. What an anticlimax!"

Woodenly, I smiled at him and then turned my eyes toward the doorway. Gideon came in and stood there a minute, watching us. The expression on his face was unfathomable. I did not see him again, because after that dance we left, and the six of us all piled into Barry's car, where I sank back into a corner hugging my secret to me. Frank, who was sitting in the front seat, swiveled himself around and scanned my face searchingly. He did not seem to like what he found there, for he frowned and turned his back again.

"You're quiet, Christy," said Margo.

"I guess I'm tired," I said, stretching as well as I could in the cramped space. I was glad to have that as an excuse. It would suffice for the sensitive ego of Barry, even if Frank was not deceived.

Anyway, tonight I did not care what Frank thought. I could only wish that this jaunt to the drive-in was over, so I could go home to my room and play "Greensleeves" on my phonograph and remember what had happened. I love him, I love him, I love him, I thought. I wanted to write it in the sky.

Chapter 12

Ordinarily, I like school, and on the first day each year I am always filled with an excitement that diminishes somewhat as time goes on, but never quite disappears; but on this, the first day of my senior year, I just wished I could go off by myself and mope. Gideon was gone, and it felt more as if he had died. But right now as I slumped down the stairs to breakfast, he was probably winging along the highway with the top down on his convertible while each turn of the wheels took him farther and farther out of my life.

Mother had the radio on in the kitchen, and between commercials and weather reports and news broadcasts, she was humming happily along with the music. I sat down at my place and looked over at her glumly.

She put a glass of juice in front of me and glanced at my face. "Christy, you look terrible this morning," she said. "I know last night was an exception, but from now on you've got to get to bed at a decent hour on school nights."

I figured that was as good a place as any to be in, but I just said, "O.K.," and picked up my glass.

"Well, well," said the syrupy voice of the radio announcer, "today is the first day of school, and after you get the kiddies off to their classes, all you mothers out there ought to sit back and take it easy for a few minutes this morning. You deserve it after the long summer vacation."

Mother lifted her orange-juice glass in a toast to the radio. "Hear, hear!" she said.

"And when you take that coffee break," the announcer went on, "don't forget to make it Beekman's Instant Coffee, the full rich coffee with the fresh, nutty flavor."

"Nutty is right," I commented sourly.

The announcer gabbled on, and I ate my breakfast. I had to force down each bite of egg and toast, but Mother was watching me balefully to see that I did, and the last thing I wanted was an argument. A record was playing on the radio, and after a while the strains of the music seeped through to my brain. They were playing *September Song*, and although it was an instrumental selection, the words started going through my mind. "And you haven't got time for the waiting game."

As a quick stab of breath caught in my throat, I put my fork down and stared ahead of me. Of course. That was it! That explained Gideon's strange action in taking me out in the garden last night. He did care for me! But he felt there was too big a difference in our ages; he was afraid he was too old to wait for me to grow up a little bit more. Oh, but that made it all the more painful, knowing for sure that he cared, because there was nothing I could do about it. I was doing my best to grow up fast, but apparently my best wasn't fast enough.

I pushed the plate away, unable to eat any more. The song went on, searing me with its sadness. Somehow I must get his address from Daddy or Julie and write to him. In some careful, unobtrusive way, I must tell him how much I loved him. If I had told him last night, would it have made a difference, I wondered. Would he have asked me then to marry him? Oh, why didn't I tell him? I had been longing to.

The song ended and the announcer came back. Unable to bear it any longer I got up and snapped off the radio.

"Now why did you do that?" Mother asked in annoyance.

"I can't stand that man," I said, going out of the room to get my school brief case.

"Well," I heard her mutter, as she turned it on again, "you might have asked me. He may be an idiot, but the music wakes me up in the morning."

On the way to Margo's house, I determined to root around Daddy's office when I got back home—if he wasn't there—and look for the address. And then, if that didn't work, I'd figure out some way to get it from Julie. She would be sure to have it.

Fortunately, not much gets done on the first day of school, so my preoccupation wasn't too much out of order. However, there are always some teachers who have to set sail immediately, and Mrs. Dikeman, the physics teacher, was one of those. Once in the middle of her lecture, she stopped talking, put on her glasses, and glared at me.

"Miss Collier, I hope you're going to be with us this year," she said sarcastically. "This is going to be a very important year for you seniors, and I don't intend to have anyone in my class who does nothing but stare out of windows."

Obediently I came to attention and realized mournfully that she was a cross I was going to have to bear stoically for the next nine months—unless, of course, by my letters to him, I could spur Gideon into coming back for me. Wouldn't that make a stir, though, if I left school and got married? Inwardly I smiled gleefully, but I was careful not to let my thoughts betray me again.

It seemed as though school would never let out, but finally it did, and I dashed home, without waiting for Margo, to make my search for the address. As I walked along the street I became conscious of a car that had slowed down and was keeping pace with me. Annoyed, I ignored it, thinking it was some boy from school trying to act smart.

"Christy," said a low masculine voice.

I stopped stock-still and stared. With my hand I stifled a little cry that had escaped me. He had come back for me! Forcing myself not to run, I went over and put my hand on the door.

"You didn't go," I said.

"No, not yet," Gideon replied, and smiled.

I stood there waiting, not sure what I ought to do next.

"Don't look so shocked," he told me, laughing. "I didn't rise up from the dead or anything. Get in. I'll take you home."

"It's only a few blocks," I said, for appearance's sake, but nevertheless I opened the door, tossed in my books, and sat down beside him.

He started the car again, but all of a sudden he looked thoughtful. "Say," he said, "there's something I'd like to talk to you about. Do you have time for a short drive? Or is your mother expecting you home right away?"

"No," I assured him, and my head was reeling. I had won! I had won! He was going to ask me to marry him.

We were both silent as he took the road through the park and then passed the outskirts of town, drove up and down wooded hills and finally came to Lake Drive. At a promontory overlooking a wide reach of the lake, Gideon stopped the car, turned off the ignition with a flick of his wrist, and leaned back. I was a little scared. What was the proper etiquette for proposals? I had never felt so alone with him before—not even last night.

He looked over at me. "I guess you're wondering why I brought you out here."

"Yes, a little," I said.

"Well, it was Frank's idea that I talk to you."

"Frank?" I was all at sea now. How was it possible that I had Frank, of all people, to thank for this exciting and frightening moment?

"And Julie backed him up on it. They said—oh, this sounds so conceited—but they said you had a crush on me."

I tried to make my face a blank. What did a person say to a thing like that? "I think *crush* is a disgusting word," I said. "I'm terribly, terribly fond of you,

Gideon, but I don't have a *crush*. I'd be ashamed to have such a thing."

"Good. I told them you were too grown-up for that, although it was almost tempting to think you did. I know I have a certain basic insecurity that forces me at times to try to make a great impression on everybody— at least, that's how Julie analyzes me—but I have a very deep affection for you, Christy, and if I ever thought I had hurt you. . . . "

"You can forget that right now," I interrupted hurriedly. "I like you exceedingly, but I don't have a crush on you, and I am not hurt about anything. I just wish you would get to the point, because I'm dying of curiosity."

Laughing softly, he took a cigarette out of the pack in his shirt pocket and lit it. "You've set my mind at ease," he said. "Well, the thing is that—due to their conviction that you were madly in love with me—Frank and Julie thought the news should come from me."

"What news are you talking about?" I asked, with a dreadful feeling of foreboding.

"Julie and I are getting married Saturday. That's why I didn't leave today."

"But you told me—"

"I *know* what I told you. But I also said I was afraid that by letting myself get roped into taking somebody to that dance, I'd find myself walking up the aisle next.

Darned if it didn't happen! I should have practiced what I preached. Last night, coming home, I found myself saying the fatal words, before I knew what I was doing."

"You knew what you were doing," I observed slowly, and little bits of memories of last night came creeping back to me. "Is that why you were so preoccupied last night? Were you planning to ask her then?"

"Yes, I suppose I was," he admitted.

"There's only one thing I don't understand," I said, groping my way through the confusion I was feeling. "Why did you kiss me?"

He looked at me sharply. "I didn't hurt you by that, did I, Christy?"

"No. Oh, no!" I said quickly. "I'm just curious, that's all. Why did you?"

I was sitting very still, and even though I might have looked relaxed, my body was stiff, and later, I found that I had cut the palm of my hand with my fingernails.

Gideon rubbed his chin musingly. "I don't know why I did," he said. "I guess the situation seemed to call for it. You looked very lovely, the music was playing, and the setting was romantic. Perhaps I felt it would have been inappropriate *not* to kiss you. I thought you felt the same way. It seemed for the moment that you and I were almost the same age. Anyway, I wasn't sure yet that I was going to ask Julie to marry me, and the feeling of good-by in the air seemed to call for a kiss. Did I do wrong, Christy? Are you still such an impressionable child that you take a light kiss seriously?"

"Of course not!" I protested hotly. "I knew you were just flirting. It's been perfectly clear to me all along that you're almost as old as my father."

"Sure I am," he said, but I could see that he didn't like being reminded of how old he was. Well, if that hurt him, I was glad. I wanted him to hurt a little, because I did—I hurt all over.

"I've sort of thought about you the way I would about a very nice uncle," I added, heaping coals of fire on his head.

"That puts me in my place," he said, grinning. "Well, I'm glad—really I am. Even if my pride is hurt a bit. You know, you're delightful, Christy. All along you've intrigued me. Someday I'll put you in a book. I've never written a straight romance, but I'm tempted, except that in the story you will pine away with unrequited love."

"How corny can you get?" I said.

Turning away, he suddenly started the car up.

"Are we going back now?" I asked. "I just remembered I have loads of homework already. And Barry promised to come over tonight if I got it done. Mother will have a fit, of course."

I was aware that I was chattering foolishly, but keeping up a constant stream of small talk was the only way to survive the trip back, and in between bits of my conversation, Gideon told me what had made him fall in love with Julie. All along he had fought it, but she was unique, he said. He had never before met anyone like her. She was so completely honest that it baffled him. Other women always fawned over him, flirted, agreed with his every opinion, but Julie's total lack of awe had put him off balance from the very first. Her very openness had made her seem mysterious, and he was sure it would take him a lifetime to get to know her.

Feeling the way I did right then about Julie, it was pretty hard to take all this adulation of her from him.

When we got to town I asked him to let me off at the park, because, I said, I had promised to meet someone there to get some homework I had missed. He was so wrapped up in his own happiness that he didn't think such a thing in the least strange, but I was glad of that. I couldn't go home yet. I watched until his car had turned the corner, and then I started to run. I ran to a place I know where no one goes very often, and hid myself deep in the bushes and let myself go. It was such a *relief* to be able to cry. I cried until there was nothing left, but it didn't really do any good. The pain wouldn't go away. It couldn't go away, because all the time there was that image of Gideon in my mind. I thought of the sure, graceful way he walked, the way his eyes crinkled up when he laughed, and the way he looked at me—all lost to me forever now. Never in my life have I felt as completely lonely as I did at that moment. I burrowed deep into the bushes. I wanted to burrow into the ground like an animal in the wintertime. I wanted to bury myself, to be dead; I never wanted to go home.

But of course I had to go home. I finally dried my face and got up and went there. I even skipped as I went up the walk, but I was also careful to go straight to my room, and I stayed there until my swollen face returned to normal. I *think* I was very blasé with everyone that night, even with Mother and Daddy, who both looked at me with concern in their faces but seemed relieved with what they found in mine. And I had to endure an evening of watching Julie and Gideon's happiness with a smile on my face, while Frank, who had also come over, stared gloomily at me from under his eyebrows.

They must never know how I felt, I thought. They would preach at me and point out that Gideon belonged to my father's generation, or else they would say it was just puppy love and would pass. They could never understand this *agony*.

And that night Julie asked me to be her maid of honor. Even that I could do.

Chapter 13

Saturday seemed to arrive awfully fast. One day it was Tuesday, when I heard the news, and the next thing it was Saturday morning, and we were getting ready to go to the church. In between there was school and loads of homework, and I went through it as though I had been hypnotized. If I had thought I would pine away like a heroine in an old sentimental novel, I was mistaken. My appetite was undiminished, and at night I slept the sleep of the just. It was unromantic that the rest of my body should be so indifferent to my heart's pain, but there it was.

On Tuesday night, after my talk with Gideon, Julie and Mother had had a conference, and it was decided that the bride would wear a suit and that the maid of honor would do very well in her last year's navy blue wool dress, so I wasn't even going to get a new outfit out of the situation.

Mother went shopping with Julie on Wednesday, and on Thursday she had a shower for her. By the time the party was over I had long since taken a bath and gotten into bed, where I propped myself up with pillows to write an English composition which was due the next morning. I had just about finished it when Julie stuck her head around the door. She smiled, but her face looked drawn and tired.

"Come on in," I said.

"My, that looks comfortable," she said and threw herself over the foot of the bed. "It *is* comfortable."

"This has been a pretty hectic week for you, hasn't it?" I commented unnecessarily.

Her answer was a small groan.

"Mother shouldn't have given a shower for you when there's so much else to do," I said.

"It was very sweet of your mother," Julie said primly.

"Oh, sure. But what use are you going to have for all that stuff, anyway, when you and Gideon are gallivanting all over the world?"

My tone must have sounded bitter, although I hadn't intended it to be, for Julie got up on one elbow and looked across the bed at me searchingly.

"I've been wanting to ask," she said, "but I didn't know how to broach the subject. *Has* this been very hard on you, Christy?"

Looking down at my composition I carefully underlined a word. "Not really," I replied.

"I wish I could believe that," she said. "I've even wondered if it's all worth it, if it means hurting you and leaving everything I've ever known."

"But you'll be coming back from time to time."

"Yes, I suppose so." Pensively she traced the pattern in the quilt with her fingernail.

"You almost sound unhappy," I observed.

She looked surprised. "Do I?" She lay there and thought for a minute. "I *thought* I was happy. Gideon's proposal was such a bolt out of the blue—I'd given up any ideas of making him care for me when I knew he was leaving the day after the dance. I was in a complete daze for a couple of days after he asked me."

"And now?"

"I don't know." She sighed and lay back with her hands clasped under her head. "It's all the excitement, I guess. I'm tired, that's all. It's funny, though, you know. Gideon's so different from the sort of man I once thought I'd marry. I have the feeling that all the rest of my life I'll be wondering what he saw in me."

To be blunt, I'd been wondering the same thing myself. If a peacock had decided to marry a little red hen it couldn't have seemed any odder than for a man like Gideon to marry someone like Julie. But I didn't say so, of course. I just said, in a careful way, that I hoped she'd never let him know she felt like that. It was strange, but I suddenly felt much older than Julie. I felt as if I were about a hundred years old.

On Friday Daddy decided to give a small stag party for Gideon at the hotel. While he was gone, Mother and I had a midnight snack before going to bed, and just as Julie had done, and as she herself had been doing all week, Mother gave me a worried look over the cups of cocoa in the kitchen.

"Do you feel all right, honey?" she asked in commiserating tones.

"I feel fine," I replied belligerently.

Naturally she would not take my word for it, and in pious accents assured me that this marriage was the best thing that could have happened as far as I was concerned.

"And as far as *they* are concerned?" I asked.

"Now what do you mean by that?" she asked.

"Julie seemed awfully tired and worried last night for a bride-to-be."

"Most girls feel uneasy before the wedding."

"I won't," I said with conviction. "I wouldn't get married if I had any doubts about myself or my future husband. I may be tired and excited before my wedding day, but one thing I do know—I'll be *sure*."

"You may be right at that," Mother said slowly, toying with her spoon. "Gideon has been a bachelor for many years. He's used to doing what he wants when he wants, while Julie is the domestic type. Still, it may work out all right—I hope it does."

"It will," I said dully. "Julie will domesticate the life right out of him, and he won't even know what happened to him."

And that was what hurt, I thought, as I got ready for bed later. Julie would change him—she already had. The very fact that now he wanted to be domesticated put him in a new light. All the glamour he had was gone. He would be just like anybody else. Not that there was anything wrong in a man's marrying a good woman and settling down and having children and worrying about drains and whether the roof leaked—but that was so ordinary and colorless. Julie had told me that Gideon was taking her to Italy for their honeymoon. After that she didn't know what they would do. But I knew. She would feel a little homesick by then, and they would come back here next summer, and by fall she would have convinced him that what he wanted most of all was a house on Walnut Street. No, Julie had no reason for doubts. She had actually gotten the kind of man she'd always wanted to marry—or he would be that kind before long. *I* would never have changed him so, for I had liked him just the way he was—gay and irresponsible and a little mad. But the romantic cavalier was dead. I missed him terribly.

The sky was overcast on Saturday morning. It matched my feelings. When we got to the church it was crowded, although both of them had wanted a small, quiet wedding. Mother left us with Frank, who was ushering, and went to sit near the front; and I waited in the vestibule with Gideon and Daddy, who was best man. Gideon paced nervously until he realized he was pacing, and stopped. "I didn't know this was going to be such a shindig," he muttered.

"It's Edna's fault," Daddy said. "If she hadn't thrown that blamed shower the other night, no one would have known about it."

From my outpost at the door I saw the car drive up. "Here come Julie and Mr. Fanelle," I said.

"We'd better go inside, Gideon," said Daddy. "It's supposed to be unlucky for the bridegroom to see the bride before the ceremony. At least, the women seem to think so."

Suffering himself to be led, the lamb meekly went in to be slaughtered, and I watched him go in a state of numb acceptance. Then I turned and faced Julie as she came up the steps.

Apparently a good night's rest had done her good. Her face looked rested, and there was a glow about it. She was wearing a fitted gray suit and a gray sailor hat with white veiling, and instead of the orchids I had expected, she had a large yellow chrysanthemum pinned to her jacket. I looked at it in surprise, and she laughed. "It's a fall wedding, isn't it?" she said.

"I like it," I told her, and added, "are you ready for the ordeal?"

She nodded, and when she answered me, her tone was confident and even buoyant. "All the doubts are gone, Christy. I'm so happy today."

"You look beautiful," I whispered, and she did. She had never looked so radiant.

"All brides are beautiful, didn't you know?" she said.

I could hear the organ playing, and then Frank stuck his head through the doorway. "Come on," he said in a hollow stage whisper, "let's get it over with." Then he disappeared.

Julie gave a half-nervous little laugh. "That boy!" she said as she took her father's arm.

It was a simple wedding and quickly over. I stood up under it pretty well, even at the last when I lifted the veil on Julie's hat so her husband could kiss her. But all weddings kill me. I don't know why. And of course, this one, above all, had a special poignancy. All through the ceremony I had to bite my tongue hard. Once I heard Mother sniffle behind me—she always cries at weddings—and it seemed to me to be the last straw. I knew that if I gave way even a little the floodgates would open and I would positively howl! Desperately I looked away from the sacrament going on in front of me and my eyes stopped at Daddy. He was watching me and looking very solemn, with his little pot belly sticking out in front of him like Tweedle-dee or Twee-dle-dum. As I looked into his eyes, I was amazed to see one of them slowly shut and then open again in a droll little wink. Instead of sobbing, I nearly laughed out loud, but I just managed to stop it in time. I felt very grateful to him for that wink. Sometimes parents *could* be understanding.

And then it was over. The words had been said, and the bride had been kissed. The organ burst into the loud chords of Mendelssohn's wedding march, and Julie, with a slightly triumphant lift to her head, went up the aisle on Gideon's arm. I wondered if all brides looked triumphant. Gideon smiled down at her, all his nerv-ousness gone, and he looked triumphant too. Well, I hoped they would be happy.

There was a small wedding breakfast afterward at the Fanelle house for the immediate family and one or two of Julie's intimate friends. When I arrived in the car with Mother and Daddy, Frank was sitting on the steps smoking his pipe, and I joined him there. He made no comment as I sat down beside him.

"Well?" I said finally.

"Well?" said Frank. He looked at me from under his eyebrows. "No tears?" he asked.

"Did you expect some?"

"Yes, I did. A few maybe."

"I'm sorry to disappoint you."

"I must say I think you're taking this very well," he said stuffily.

"What'd you suppose I'd do, lie on the floor and scream?"

"Sarcasm doesn't fool me one bit," said Frank, and then he changed the subject abruptly. "I hate weddings," he said.

"Why?"

"They reek of convention. All that organ music and women sobbing. I've never liked Gideon particularly, but believe me, my heart went out to him today. It's inhuman to put a man through that."

"It seems to me he put himself into that position," I commented dryly.

"Coming from you, Miss Collier, that sounds suspiciously like a catty remark."

"*Touché!*" I said.

"But there's something even worse than weddings,"

he went on as if to himself, "and that's funerals. Have you ever been to a funeral, Christy?"

"No," I said uncomfortably.

"Now, there's a barbaric custom for you. It really goes back to pagan times. We don't put food in with the corpses any more or burn the widow on the funeral pyre, but some of the social customs we have now are just about as bad. I find funerals fascinating, however, but weddings merely bore me."

"Do you know something, Frank?" I said. "*You* bore *me.*"

I got up and went in the house. He was in a very exasperating mood.

However, I did notice that his dislike of weddings stopped at the church door. He had no antipathy to wedding breakfasts. The whole party watched in wide-eyed amusement as that skinny boy, oblivious to all, put away two grapefruit halves, three eggs, eight slices of Canadian bacon, three pieces of toast, and five pancakes, smothered in butter and syrup.

Frank pushed his chair away from the table. "I'm full," he said mildly, and then looked astonished as everyone hooted with laughter.

"Do you have some secret sorrow, Frank, that drives you to eat?" Gideon asked him across the table.

Frank glowered for a moment, and then thought bet-

ter of it. He smiled mysteriously—or at least, he seemed
to think it was mysterious.

"I expect to outgrow it," was all he said, and this
made everyone laugh again.

Gideon took advantage of the distraction to look
questioningly at Julie, who nodded. They were going
to leave. Suddenly things began happening very fast.
People started getting up from the table as Julie went
upstairs, and Mother went with her. Men were milling
about the hallways, and some younger boy cousins of
Julie's went out to put a *Just Married* sign and tin cans
on the rear bumper of Gideon's car. Then the happy
couple appeared on the porch, and there was a lot of
kissing and hugging. I tried to stay out of it, but Julie
came over to me, and I felt her cool kiss on my cheek.

"Have a nice year," she whispered. "We'll be back
next summer, if not sooner."

I thought I couldn't have cared less, but I didn't say
so. And then I felt a sudden pang at the thought of los-
ing Julie—not Gideon, Julie. A man had come between
us, but the past could not be erased entirely. Impul-
sively, I put my hand over her gloved one.

"I'll miss you, Julie," I said. "But please be happy."

"Oh, I will—I am," she breathed. Then she put her
arms around me and hugged me. "I hate to leave you
somehow. You'll be all grown-up and changed when
I see you again."

I wondered what she meant by that, but there was no time for me to ask her. Other people were pressing for the last moments of her attention, kissing her and pumping Gideon's hand. And then they were walking toward the car, where the boys were just finishing the sign and the tin cans. Gideon chased them away, shaking his finger at them, and he removed the decorations, throwing them on the grass. Still smiling, he got in the car beside his wife, they waved, and then they were gone. They looked glad to be leaving, and Gideon hadn't even said good-by to me.

People started going home after that, and Mother and Daddy headed toward our car. Frank stopped me as I followed them. "Can I walk you home?" he asked.

"O.K.," I said, and motioned to Mother and Daddy, who went on without me.

We walked slowly as a watery sun picked its way through the clouds. "Happy is the bride the sun shines on," I quoted.

"Um," said Frank.

"I forgot. That was the wrong thing to say to someone who doesn't approve of weddings."

But Frank had already expressed his opinion on that subject and did not seem to want to pursue it further. He looked at me. "How do you feel now?" he asked.

"Everyone's been asking me that this week. I'm getting a little tired of it."

"Well, you looked a little bleak several times today."

"Weddings always make me sad."

"*This* one in particular."

I rewarded him with a scornful look, but it seemed to goad him on.

"Was it very hard to convince Gideon that you didn't have a crush on him? It must have been an awful blow to his pride."

"Why do you hate him so much? What has he ever done to you?"

Frank slumped his shoulders, looking for all the world like a woeful basset hound. "He ruined things for me, that's why. He deliberately set out to make your little heart flutter, and he succeeded. I didn't find it out right at first. That night I met you I really thought you were interested in me, and again, the night you almost agreed to be my girl. But all the time, he's been sitting at one side, gloating because I was miserable, which made me all the less attractive. No one can be attractive when he's miserable."

"I know," I agreed, but actually, this was the first time I'd really been fully conscious of the fact that Frank might be unhappy too.

"Right now you're probably thinking that you hate Gideon," he said. "Why can't you be indifferent to him? Then I'd have a chance."

I looked at him helplessly. He sounded so pathetic.

"Nothing lasts forever," I said. "Not even love—not when you've lost the person you love. But please don't push things, Frank. I think I *am* indifferent to him now, but at the same time there's nothing to take his place. Anyway, you and I both have years and years of education before us yet. If I fell in love with you now, I probably *wouldn't* love you in five years. Have you ever thought of that?"

His face brightened. "No, I hadn't. But you know, you've got a point there." He went on walking ahead, with his face all lit up as though this possibility gave him a marvelous new bit of philosophy to mull over.

Laughing, I had to run to catch up with him. "Maybe in five years or so, when we're both out of college, you'll be so sick of me that you'll wonder why you ever acted like this. And perhaps, then, I'll be wild about you. 'Oh, Frank, darling,' I'll say, 'how can you be so cruel?' "

He laughed too, and stopping, he half put his arms around me and hugged me in the silliness of the moment. But right after that his expression changed back to the usual serious one.

"Ever since I was eight years old," he said, "I've known I wanted to be an archaeologist. Not once has it ever occurred to me to want anything different. You'd better resign yourself, Christy. Once I make up my mind about something I never change it."

I backed away from him, feeling trapped all of a sudden. I felt surrounded by his singleness of purpose, as though it were a warm stuffy cloak that blotted out life and sunlight and half-smothered me.

"No," I said. "You must forget about me, Frank."

We were at my house by this time, and I ran in, leaving him standing near the curb in front of Daddy's car. As I looked back I could see him looking a little lost for a second, until he put his hands in his pockets and walked away. And then, perversely, I wanted to run after him and put my arm through his. He was such a strange boy, but I knew I liked him better than Barry or any other boy in town. If only he didn't have such a one-track mind!

Chapter 14

Life went on, and outwardly, anyway, it was just as though Gideon had never come into our lives; everyone made a special point of not mentioning him to me. I smiled wistfully to myself, knowing, if they didn't, that I did not need any remarks from them to remind me of him.

I had hoped that the numb feeling I had had at the wedding would change to indifference, but it didn't. Instead, it became a sad, lost feeling that now seemed to be a part of me. I must admit that I indulged it frequently. When I had the house to myself, I would go to my room and put the record of "Greensleeves" on the portable phonograph and sit with Gideon's note in my hand. At other times I got poetry out of the library. Dorothy Parker and Emily Dickinson I read over and over.

There were a few post cards and letters from Julie. Gideon never wrote, but Julie would always add at the end, "Gideon sends everybody his love." I wondered if he had, or if she was just being polite to cover his apathy toward us all, now that he was away from us. She wrote to us about Rome, Venice, and, most of all, Naples. "Capri is paradise. I wish you could see it, Christy. And I'm writing Frank in detail about Pompeii. I don't think I ever want to come home." Could it be that she was proving me wrong, that she would not domesticate him, but would instead be changed by him? I realized now that I did not want to be wrong. Now I knew that it would be easier to bear if Gideon changed. Then I could think of him as dead, and I would get over it.

Frank came to see me as often as he could, but after college opened I saw him less frequently. He gave up his library job, except for Saturdays, and I was able to indulge in poetry without any chance of his seeing it.

October turned the trees to torches of yellow and scarlet under a vivid blue sky, and Margo and I watched Barry and Steve play football on Saturday afternoons. At school I joined the Camera Club and learned how to develop my own pictures, and I was elected to the Prom Committee. Life went on.

One Saturday night Mother and Daddy went out, leaving me alone in the house to play "Greensleeves" to my heart's content. Barry had gone off with the football team for a game away from home and had not come back yet, and I had not seen Frank for a week, as he had been busy studying. It was the first week end in a long time when I had not had a date, but I didn't mind. It was nice to be able to play the record loud and to read poetry as I listened to it. I was right in the middle of "I measure every grief I meet," when I became aware that someone was calling my name. Opening the window wider, I stuck my head out and saw Frank standing in front of the house.

"Christy?"

"I'll be right down."

I hated to go. It was a nuisance to have my mood destroyed.

I sat down beside him on the steps, buttoning up my sweater against the autumn coolness.

"Hi," I said. "How are your studies coming along?"

"Fine," said Frank. He was his usual gloomy self. "Was that 'Greensleeves' I heard you playing?"

"What if it was?" I asked, on my guard now.

"Gideon gave you that, didn't he? I heard him say

something to Julie about it the day he bought it for you."

"Now that I remember it, I think he did. It's my favorite song, though. Always has been."

"You make me sick," Frank said succinctly.

"That's interesting," I said, trying to play it lightly. "Maybe it's some kind of an allergy."

"You're like a typical old maid of the nineteenth century. The kind who sat around all her life feeling delicate and reading old love letters tied up in blue ribbon, because she lost the only man she ever loved."

"Very funny," I said, but I was not laughing.

"I'd feel sorry for you," he went on relentlessly, "but I can't. How can anyone feel sorry for you? You *enjoy* being miserable. I'll bet if you tried to right now you couldn't even remember what Gideon looks like."

"I could too," I said. Hadn't I been looking at his picture earlier that evening?

"All you're doing is putting on a big act."

"I don't think I want to talk to you, Frank," I said, and I got up.

He arose too and looked at me squarely. "I don't think I want to talk to *you*," he said.

"And just what do you mean by that?"

"I think it's pretty plain. I'm tired of all your posing and sighing over that sap. Even though I did tell you I never change my mind about anything, I *have* changed it about you. You're not worth thinking about. Go back to your room and play your song and cry over old Gideon. I don't care. And I won't bother you any more either. Someday I'll find a girl who's interested in *me*."

Turning on his heel, he left me standing there without giving me a chance to think of a reply. What could I say anyhow? He had had the last word. Maybe he even deserved to. But still, I was filled with frustrated anger. I ran back into the house and slammed the door so that the windows shook, and went to my room as fast as I could, where I turned on the record player to the peak of its volume. The window was still open. I hoped he could hear it. That would show him what I cared about his opinion!

The record whirled to a close, sweet and loud and with violins piercing the night. There were no words being sung, but I knew the words. "Greensleeves, now farewell, adieu."

Anyway, who cares about you, Frank Fanelle, I thought. I contemplated playing it again just to show him. I lifted the arm to do so, and then thought better of it. I was getting a little tired of it anyway. Besides, maybe he was right. Maybe? I knew darn well he was. That was the point that nagged me. He had had the last word, and there was no comeback for me, because I knew he was right.

If only I could prove to him that I was not a Victorian old maid. But I never could now. Frank always said what he meant, and he wasn't coming back. He had given me plenty of chances to be his friend, and I had been sickening, just as he said. But, I thought, I could prove it to myself. Curiously, I looked at the record as though it were alive. And then, almost frightened, I put the needle down on it and lowered the sound to a more reasonable pitch. Each sweet measure was as familiar to me as the tone of my own voice. But I *was* tired of it. How long had I been tired of it without knowing I was? Listening to it to the end, I was struck by something else. It did not mean anything to me any longer. It was just a nice song, nothing more.

Taking it off the turntable, I held it in my hands for a moment, until finally, closing my eyes, I broke it cleanly over my knee, and sat looking at the two halves. As I stared down at them, a great weight seemed to lift from me, and for the first time in months I felt free. To prove it to myself still more, I calmly tore up Gideon's note into small pieces and placed them in a pile on top of the broken record. I was over it! As easily as that! But Frank was not there to see.

Monday after school Barry asked me to go to the senior prom with him in January, and without hesitation I agreed. Although I had planned on asking Frank to go with me, that was out of the question now. And to re-assert my independence of him, I had my hair cut again—short—because I knew he didn't like it that way.

Later in the week Margo told me that she had been talking to Milly, who had confessed to having asked him to the prom herself. Frank had said he would go with her.

"I was sure Frank would want to go with you," said Margo.

"No, I'm going with Barry. Frank and I are *phftt*."

"Oh, Christy, not again!"

"I'm afraid so," I admitted, and put a hand to my head. I was more glad than ever that I'd had my hair cut. "Only this time it's for keeps. You know how stubborn Frank is. He said he never wanted to see me again, and of course, he meant it."

"Boy! You sure do have the growing pains," she said. "Sometimes I get to thinking that life is pretty trying for me, but then all I have to do is think about you, and I'm comforted at how normal I am. What happened this time?"

"The same old thing."

"You mean Gideon? But he's gone!"

"Not for me he wasn't—at least, not until Saturday night. Frank caught me playing a record Gideon gave me, and he said I acted like an old maid pining away over a man who'd never cared for me in the first place—

he didn't say that exactly, but that's what he meant. And the worst part of it is, that it's true. I've been behaving like a perfect fool."

"Yes, you have."

"But I'm over it now, Margo, really over it. If Gideon came back today, it wouldn't matter. I don't hate him; I don't miss him; I just don't *care* any more."

"Thank goodness for that. But it certainly is a shame about Frank. He's an awfully odd boy in a lot of ways, but at the same time he's the most attractive man to come to town in ages—including Gideon Myles. I don't know what it is. You couldn't call him handsome—he's awkward and gruff and full of opinions. But he reminds me of a mixture of Abraham Lincoln and Lord Byron."

"Byron! Frank isn't a poet."

"But he looks like one." Margo sighed. "I'm very fond of Steve, but if Frank had ever given me a tumble, I think I'd have lost all my senses. To tell you the truth, Christy, when it seemed to me that you didn't care much for him, I went to the library a couple of times and tried, but he looked right through me. Oh, he was polite enough, but he had you on his mind. It was very easy to tell, because that was all he wanted to talk about. Well, anyway, I'm glad you never had a crush on him. I have a feeling that that dark, brooding stranger would be a lot harder to get over than Gideon Myles ever could be."

"Dark, brooding stranger," I repeated. "That's a pretty good way to describe him."

"Uh *huh!*" said Margo. "I've seen him look at you that way lots of times when you weren't noticing. Even though it wasn't me, it gave me shivers. I think Frank has great depths in him."

The bell clanged in the school building to announce the end of the lunch period. We had been sitting on the steps in front of the building.

"Time to go back to the salt mines," said Margo, gathering herself up. "Well, *c'est la vie*. At any rate, this is the last year of it. College won't be half as regimented."

"It'll be a lot harder," I reminded her, as we walked back to our classroom. "And thank goodness I'm all settled down now. I've got to get that physics grade up or I won't even get into college."

The speech was mother to the resolution. It just occurred to me at that minute that I was letting a very important year of high school slip by. To the surprise and gratification of my parents, I began attending to my studies much more diligently than in the past. In the first place, I really did want to get into college, and in the second place, it kept my mind off the hurt Frank's brush-off had given my pride.

Since there was no reason for our paths to cross, I never saw him. The only place I could have seen him was in the library on Saturday, and I kept away from there then. I told myself I didn't want to see him anyway. I was well rid of his tiresome conversation and his possessiveness. Nevertheless, Margo's comments stuck in my mind. The dark, brooding stranger. In spite of everything, I began to think of him like that.

I took the poetry books back to the library one night, and while I was there I took Byron off the shelf. There was a picture of the poet as a frontispiece. Did Frank look like that? Well, maybe.

Tucking the book under my arm, I browsed over toward the biographies and found a life of Byron to read along with the poems. It wasn't because of Frank, of course, but merely because Margo had always claimed that Byron was romantic, and I wanted to see for myself.

On my way out, I glanced over the special section where popular books were kept for the convenience of the borrowers, and there among the murder mysteries and best-selling novels of a few months back, I saw a title that caught my eye. It was called *Digging in the Past.* I pulled it out quickly and found that, just as I suspected, it was about archaeology. I looked around to see if there was anyone I knew in the library. There wasn't. Even Emma was absent that evening. Putting it with the other two books on my arm, I walked over to the lending desk and had all three stamped out, and as I left the library I felt almost guilty. But after all, I had a right to read whatever I wanted to, didn't I?

The October night was cold, and I could see my breath as I trudged home. Passing the street where the Fanelles lived, I glanced down toward the house and could see through the trees a light shining from an upstairs window. Frank was probably studying. He wasn't like me; he didn't moon about and sigh over unattainable things when he should be at his books. He knew what he wanted, and I had a feeling he would succeed. Having me in his life would just distract him, and he had sense enough to see that his future was more important to him than wasting his time and emotion over a silly high-school girl who didn't know her own mind.

But much as I had missed the excitement of having Gideon around, I now missed the companionship of Frank. It would be nice now to have a boy like him for a friend, someone whose silences were not uncomfortable pauses and whose enthusiasms might interest me enough to send me delving into obscure library books. For the first time, I admitted to myself that I wanted him back the way he was before, not for any selfish reasons, such as fear of unpopularity—I did not need Frank around to make me feel popular; there were plenty of boys for dates—but because I liked him.

I supposed that sometime I would run into him. It

would probably be unexpected, and I told myself I ought to prepare myself for that. How embarrassing it would be if I were to look startled or ill at ease! Suppose he came around that corner right now with Milly beside him? I would have to smile, and maybe I would wave carelessly and say, "Hi," or something and keep on walking, perfectly poised. That seemed sort of inadequate, but it was all I could think of. It certainly was a moment to dread, but if I kept practicing, perhaps I could carry it off all right. But whatever I did, he must never know or even suspect that I missed him or cared about him in the slightest. After all, I still had some pride left.

Chapter 15

"Maid of Athens, ere we part,
Give, oh, give me back my heart!
Or, since that has left my breast,
Keep it now, and take—the rest!"

Reading Byron made me think of ancient Greece, and ancient Greece made me think of archaeology, and archaeology made me think of—made me think that it really was a fascinating subject.

When Margo discovered me reading the life of Byron, she was delighted at the thought of having someone share her interest in him, and we had long discussions about him.

But while I ate up the facts of the poet's life with relish, and even a slight case of shock, I was very careful to keep the archaeology book to myself and see that it was hidden in the bottom of my drawer at home. I wasn't ashamed to be reading it, but I knew people would get the wrong idea. *Digging in the Past* was a popular approach to the story of archaeology, but it was just right for someone who knew nothing about it. It told about Schliemann and Troy, about the discovery of King Tut's tomb, and the labyrinth at Crete, and of Stephens and Catherwood in Central America; and as I pored over it, I thought of how useful a good photographer would be on one of those expeditions. I was intrigued with the possibilities of flying over an area to take pictures which would show by the terrain and the way the grass grew whether anything was buried underneath. And I wondered how much flying lessons would cost at Peabody Airport.

I was so excited about my new discoveries that I longed to talk about them with someone, but even with Margo I had to be reticent. I could imagine what she would say: "You *do* like Frank. A girl doesn't read up on a man's favorite subject unless she's interested in him. Oh, you poor fish!" But it wasn't like that at all. Maybe I did take the book out of the library because I was thinking a little bit about Frank, but now I really was caught up in it, and the only thing he had to do with it was that he would be the one person who would understand my fascination.

October was nearly over. Gusts of wind tore through the maple tree in the back yard, so that each day the limbs were a little more bare than they were the day before. Then the bright weather broke one Friday, and a storm ripped through town. Shrieking winds, like frantic witches, rattled the windows and doors and whined around the house, and sheets of rain pelted down. On the way to school Margo and I found our umbrellas useless and finally had to wrap our raincoats around us tightly, clutch our books to us, and run, laughing all the way. The storm abated somewhat by the afternoon, but it still rained steadily. The sidewalks were brown with the fallen leaves plastered to them, and you could see the gray sky through the clean, quivering branches of the trees.

My books were due at the library, and I decided to go, more because of the exciting weather than in spite of it.

"I think you're very foolish to go out in this rain when you don't have to," said Mother. She was sitting in front of the fireplace with one leg tucked under her and a book in her lap.

"I like it," I said. "Besides," I added, glancing at the window, "it seems to have stopped. There's a mist coming up."

"All the more reason to stay home. A night like this makes me want to sit by the fire and eat apples and read."

"I know," I agreed, "and I'll do that when I get back."

"Oh, I nearly forgot." She jumped out of her chair and started rooting around the desk. "There was a letter for you today—from Julie."

She handed it to me, and I put my books on the floor, being careful that the titles weren't exposed, and read it, half sitting on the arm of Daddy's chair.

As I read I could feel my eyes widening, and I finally squealed, "Listen to this! 'Well, I have been learning what it is to be married to a writer. Sometimes he is like the man who wasn't there. Even when he isn't working at his desk, he goes into sudden trances, which, I suppose, are something I will have to get used to. Anyhow, I have just read the results of the past six weeks' labor. It is the very rough first few chapters and outline of a novel about a man who revisits the scenes of his childhood. Even at this unpolished stage, I can see that it may be the best thing he has ever done. It is much more profound than most of his work and seems to have been torn from some place deep within him that I didn't know existed.

" 'However, the main thing I wanted to tell you is that there is a character in the story who might be you. She is sixteen, full of growing pains, and very, very lovable. Although Gideon calls her Betsy in the story, I have been unable to think of her as anything but Christy. There are some fictional additions, of course, but the essence is you. It is a very accurate portrait, sometimes too accurate, for she falls in love with the older man, but it is so honest and full of affection that I don't think you will be offended.

" 'From the looks of things, Gideon was observing more about all of us this summer than any of us suspected, but of all the characters, Betsy is the one who stands out most vividly and most true to life. Gideon says he loves her more than any character he has ever "created"—and the quotation marks are his. I wanted you to know that, too. At any rate, the book needs a lot of work yet, and it may be months before he has it in the hands of his publisher, but I thought I'd write and warn you. I hope you'll be pleased, not angry, for it really is a very great compliment.' "

I looked up, entranced. "There's more," I said, "but it's about Italy, not the book. Well, what do you think?"

Daddy looked up at me over his glasses. "The question is: what do *you* think: Shall we sue him?"

"Oh, Daddy," I said, "*hon*estly!"

"What your father means," Mother said carefully, "is that we hope it hasn't—well, hasn't affected you in any way."

"Of course, it's affected me. I think it's wonderful!" I whirled about the room ecstatically. "*I'm* in a book! Not many girls can say that!" But then I came to a stop and said more seriously, "I know what you're thinking, though. You're afraid I'll be in love with him again. Well, I am," and seeing the expression on their faces at that, I laughed. "Not the way you think," I said. "I'll always be a little bit in love with him, though, the way you are with an actor or, well, a writer. Only this writer came into my life, and he couldn't leave it just the way he found it, now could he? The best thing is that he didn't forget me; I thought he had. And that's all I wanted really—just to be remembered."

"Oh, Christy!" Mother started to laugh, but she seemed to be half crying.

"What's the matter?"

"Sometimes you act almost grown-up."

"Mother, let's face it," I said, picking up my books and buttoning my raincoat. "To you, I'll never be completely grown-up. You'll always put that 'almost' in there."

"Of course," she said, and as I started to go out the door, she called after me, "put on your galoshes."

"It isn't raining," I called back, and closed the door behind me.

I felt like dancing as I went down the steps. The rain *had* stopped and the wind, too. The soft mist closed about me, and it felt cool on my shorn head. Putting up my free hand, I could feel the drops of mist clinging to it already. It seemed rather romantic, and as I thought of that, I also wondered giddily what Gideon had said about me in his book. Oh, I couldn't wait to tell Margo about it! I would be sort of famous, but uncomfortably, I also felt something like a case history, too. I hoped he hadn't seen through me too well. If people recognized me in the book, it would be rather like walking around stark naked.

After groping my way through the quickly gathering fog, I at last saw the lights of the library shining cozily ahead of me. Someone was walking in front of me, a dark figure in the white atmosphere. As I drew closer, I could see that it was a man who was also turning into the library. He must have heard me following him up the steps, for he stopped and held the door open for me. The light from the doorway was glowing and cheerful, and it fell upon his face as I looked up to thank him. Then I stopped short with the words unsaid and my mouth still open. It was Frank.

We recognized each other at the same time. Frank's first impulse obviously was to let the door go for a second, but he quickly recovered and opened it again with an awkward motion. I walked past him stiffly and knew that all my resolutions to be poised when I saw him had gone straight down the drain. "Thank you," I said.

Quickly I went to the return desk and, standing with my back half turned to Frank, I waited in embarrassment for Emma Morrison to come and take my books. She was busy with someone who was apparently trying to get a current book with a long waiting list. She seemed to be having a hard time convincing the woman that the book was in great demand and not readily available. I tried to conceal my impatience, but I felt very ill at ease. Frank was standing right behind me.

Finally the woman filled out a reserve card and Emma came over to me, smiling apologetically. "Sorry to keep you standing there so long, Christy." And then, glancing at Frank, she added, "Hello, Frank. Are you on a busman's holiday?"

"I wanted to look something up," I heard him mutter. "Thought I'd return this while I was here."

Emma took my books. I hoped she wouldn't notice them, but the library was almost empty, and she must have needed some amusement. I leaned against the desk, clutching the edge.

"Hmm," she said. "I see you're on a Byron kick. Have you tried Swinburne, Christy? I loved him when I was your age."

"No. I'll look him up."

I held my breath. She was looking at the third book.

"*Digging in the Past!*" she exclaimed. "Why, I didn't know you were interested in archaeology too. Frank must have started you on this."

"No," I protested. "Oh, no." I would have liked to sink through the floor. Involuntarily, my eyes turned to Frank and then retreated hastily. That dark, brooding stranger look was on his face. It was impossible to know what he was thinking. It was crazy, but my heart was thudding in utter confusion.

When Emma handed me my card, I snatched it quickly and hurried toward the poetry section. I was glad she had mentioned Swinburne, at least, for it was the only book I could think of at the moment. Nervously, I scanned the names, but there was no Swinburne among them. Starting at the top of the shelf, I went through them again, running my finger along the books. Someone must have borrowed it.

For a few minutes I had been aware that Frank was standing beside me, but I pretended not to notice. Finally he said, "Are you looking for Swinburne?"

"Yes."

"You won't find him there. Those are American poets. Swinburne was English." He pointed to the shelves next to the ones I had been looking at.

"Oh," I said. "Thank you." It occurred to me to say that he needn't bother showing me, that he wasn't working there tonight, but I decided that that would be making too much of an issue of the matter. As I pulled out the volume I directed a veiled glance at Frank. He had taken a book himself from somewhere and was sitting down at a table and opening his notebook. It seemed to me that there was a flicker at the corners of his mouth as though he was trying not to smile at something. It was annoying to think that he knew I was uncomfortable, and I thought it was very ungentlemanly of him to enjoy the knowledge. If it wasn't for the fact that he knew how much I loved to browse around the library, I would have left then and there, but leaving now would prove to him that I felt humiliated, so I decided to stay. Besides, I wanted to get a supply of books for the week end. I liked poetry, but not a continual diet of it.

Idly, I leafed through the Swinburne. The gist of some of the lines floated up through my perturbed thoughts, and grinning, I wondered if Emma had read it lately. She must have forgotten, but I was glad she had recommended it.

Since Frank already knew I was cultivating an interest in his favorite subject, I figured the harm had been done and I didn't have to make a secret of taking out another book on archaeology, as well as one on ancient history, to explain some of the things I hadn't understood. After searching for a while in parts of the library I wasn't very familiar with, I found the books I

wanted at last and took them to the desk. Emma looked
at them with interest, but all she said was, "Very com-
mendable," and let it go at that, for which I was just
as glad.

I said good night and left. Outside, the night was
mistier than ever. As I stood on the bottom library step
buttoning my raincoat I could only see a few inches in
front of me. The thick fog made everything look
strange, and I wondered if I would be able to find my
way home. Then behind me, the library door burst
open and Frank came stumbling down the steps so fast
that he almost knocked me over as he rushed right into
me.

"Christy! I thought you were gone."

"I will be in a minute."

"I mean I thought I'd better walk you home. You'll
get lost."

"I don't think so."

"Just the same, I think I ought to." He fell into step
beside me and soon we were enveloped by the white-
ness. When we came to the corner I missed the curb
entirely and would have fallen if Frank hadn't grabbed
me. "See what I mean," he said. Putting his notebook
in his pocket and taking my books, he tucked my arm
into his and held on to it tightly.

We did not hurry. We had to be careful anyway, or
we would have walked right into a tree. Neither of us

spoke for a while. I think he felt shy; I know I did. But at the same time it felt wonderfully natural to be with Frank again. I was happy that we had to walk slowly, for I wanted to prolong the time with him as long as possible.

Suddenly he asked me bluntly, "Why are you reading up on archaeology?"

"I just happened to see that book, and I got curious."

"No other reason?"

"No."

"Oh. Well, I'm just as glad you discovered it for yourself. Do you like it?"

"I think it's *fascinating*, Frank."

He stopped walking. "I knew you'd think so, once you got over being stubborn about it."

"I wasn't being stubborn. You were trying to cram it down my throat."

"I suppose I was," he said dully. "In that case, I'm sure you weren't thinking of me at all when you started reading it."

"Maybe I was thinking of you just a little."

His fingers tightened around mine. "I'm glad," he said gruffly.

Shrouded in the mist, we began walking again but more slowly than ever and very close together.

"I feel as if we were the only people left in the world," Frank said.

"Yes," I said, and then, taking my pride in my hands, I added, "I've missed you, Frank."

Again the fingers tightened. "Not half as much as I've missed you," he said, and looked straight ahead of him.

As we passed a street light, I permitted myself the luxury of studying his face. He had taken off his glasses, probably because of the weather, and his face had that defenseless look it always got without them. But I also noticed how his chin jutted out stubbornly and the way his black hair grew in two lines down the back of his neck and under his collar. He certainly was not handsome. In fact, he was more like a grizzly bear. I wondered what it was about him that was so attractive. Maybe it was the smoldering depths in him that Margo had suspected.

Deliberately, he turned his head and looked at me. "Why are you staring at me?" he asked.

"Because I don't think I ever really looked at you before."

"I'm ugly," he said scowling.

"You think that because you only see what's in the mirror."

"That's enough for me," he commented a trifle savagely, and he stopped walking again. "There's something I'd like to talk to you about. Would you like to go over to Perry's for a Coke? We could talk there."

"I'd love it," I agreed.

Carefully we groped our way across the street and downtown again, toward Perry's. There were a few people on the streets, but mostly we had them to ourselves. In the business district neon lights glowed pinkly against the fog, and Perry's was deserted except for Mr. Perry, who was sitting behind the counter listening to the radio.

Frank ordered two Cokes and brought them back to the booth in the rear of the store. We sat there sipping through the straws and feeling a little embarrassed, now that we could see each other clearly.

Finally I asked, "What did you want to talk about, Frank."

"Gideon Myles," he said, looking across at me squarely.

"What about him?"

"Are you over him? I know it's insane to ask, but I've got to know."

"Yes," I said, "there's no doubt about it. I am." I smiled to myself. How could I possibly still care for Gideon when all I'd thought of for the past month was Frank himself? "But," I added cautiously, "I think there's something you ought to know, if you don't know it already. Today I had a letter from Julie, and she said that Gideon is putting me in a book—he told me he might, but I didn't believe him then."

Frank digested this news for a minute and then said sarcastically, "What do you think about being a character in a book by Gideon Myles?"

"Why, I'm excited, of course. I can't help wondering what he has said. Perhaps I won't like it at all, but whatever he says, it won't make any difference about my feeling for Gideon personally. I'll always like him. But I'm not in love with him any more. Maybe I never was. It's more as if I was in love with the idea of being in love with him."

"Do you mean that? Why, that's what I always thought, but I was afraid to say so for fear you'd get mad. Maybe now there's a chance for me." He said the last words with a rising inflection, a little questioningly.

"I don't think you have any right to ask that—not after giving me the brush-off the way you did."

"I had to. Someone had to shock you out of your decline," he said, with a grumpy look at me from under his eyebrows.

"I would have come out of it sooner or later, but that may have helped. Actually, I was getting awfully tired of 'Greensleeves.' And that night after you left in such a huff, I—I broke the record, and it didn't matter."

"You did it on purpose?"

I nodded, and Frank gazed across at me steadily. A

little smile played over his face. "I wish I could have seen that," he said.

We smiled bashfully at each other, and I was conscious that for the first time since I had known him I did not feel comfortable in Frank's presence. Strangely enough, I did not mind—it was a delicious kind of shyness.

"I suppose you're going to the prom with Barry," he said at last. "Doggone it, do you think we'll ever get to go to a dance together?"

"Well, I heard you had already been spoken for," I reminded him.

"I don't want to go with Milly. You know how I feel about dances generally anyway, but you're always driving me into these things. I don't even like her very much."

"I hate her!" I said vehemently.

"You do?" he said, and he repeated it. "You do? Not only do you hate Milly, but you suddenly like archaeology?" Frank looked as if he could have soared right out of the booth. Then he added thoughtfully, "And being a photographer, you'd be a great help to someone on an expedition."

"I thought of that," I said. I brought up the subject of taking pictures from the air, and we discussed the possibilities of flying lessons at the airport if we could save up enough money.

"You know," Frank said, "I think we would make a great team. It's good if a wife can go along with her husband on archaeological trips."

"Are you proposing to me, Frank?"

He gave me another one of his rare grins. "No. We have too many years to wait yet. But keep it in mind, will you?"

"I'll do that," I said. "But I thought you didn't approve of weddings. You implied that they were archaic social customs and terribly boring."

"I still think so," he admitted, a little chagrined, "but in this case, I'd overlook that."

Our eyes met over the table, and even with Mr. Perry so near and the radio blaring, I felt very much alone with him.

"I love you, Christy," he said simply.

The phrase caught me by surprise. No one had ever said that to me before.

"I love you too," I whispered, and as I said the words, I suddenly doubted if the world would ever be quite the same place again.

Frank's breath caught for a minute, and then he said gruffly, "Let's get out of this place."

We left Perry's in a kind of dream and stumbled out into the white night. As we left the neon signs behind, the mist surrounded us again, hiding all the world.

We walked very close together and occasionally the

rough sleeve of his jacket brushed against my cheek. When we reached the place where once he had almost kissed me, Frank stopped as though remembering, and he shifted the books he was carrying for me from one arm to the other. Finding that no better, he shifted them back again. Finally, he gave up on it altogether and with more force than finesse grabbed me with the free arm while the books in his other arm jabbed into me uncomfortably. His kiss was rough and awkward, but in spite of the interfering books, it left me oddly shaken. Frank let go of me abruptly. "That wasn't very romantic," he muttered.

I didn't know what to say. Somehow it didn't seem ladylike to tell him I'd liked it. Instead, I reached up and planted a gentle kiss of my own on his damp scratchy cheek.

"What was that for?"

"Because you are very sweet," I said.

Very tenderly then he put his free hand on the back of my head and pressed his face against mine, and I felt his fingers in my short hair.

"Christy," he said softly.

"Yes?"

"Do me a favor, will you?"

"What is it?"

"Let your hair grow."

"Yes, Frank," I whispered meekly.

That was three months ago, and since then, nothing has changed. I go out with other boys, of course, because Mother and Daddy won't let me go steady with Frank, but that doesn't matter. He knows I'm really his girl. There is something I will never tell him, though, for he would never understand. Last week I was listening to the radio in my room and doing my homework. All of a sudden I heard a song I had thought I was tired of. It was "Greensleeves." And for a while everything that happened last summer came back to me in a flash. I know I love Frank and always will, but there will also be times when I'll think of Gideon with a kind of sad, sweet poignancy. Frank, I know, is here, and he is real, and we have many things to look forward to, but this other thing is real in its way too. It isn't that I'm still in love with Gideon, but just that I know I'll never forget. Nevertheless, I do feel guilty about it at times. However, as Margo would say—*c'est la vie.*

I

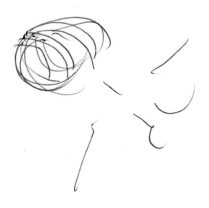